Kaleidoscopes in the Dark

Dark short stories in technicolour

B. G. Rogers

Published by B.PRESS
First published 2022
Copyright © B. G. Rogers 2022
bgrogers.com

A catalogue record for this book is available in the National Library of New Zealand.

ISBN 978-0-473-64879-4 (Softcover)
ISBN 978-0-473-64709-4 (Epub)
ISBN 978-0-473-64710-0 (Kindle)
ISBN 978-0-473-64707-0 (Softcover - POD)

Find light even in darkness

Contents

Overdue

PLEASE READ THIS. If you've found this, then there's hope you'll find us. Or at least I can prevent you from falling into the same fate. I imagine you there, sitting in one of those awful beige chairs, the sun striking through the library windows. There's probably a tourist whinging about the lack of free Wi-Fi and at least three students poring over English Language textbooks.

You see, I used to sit exactly where you're sitting now. Leafing through the magazines and books and harassing the staff to order in the latest 'it' bestseller. Which reminds me – do not tell the staff about this note. They could be in on it. I don't know. But for your own safety, for mine, don't tell them. Please.

I'm not sure what you can do, or who you can tell. So I will ask you only one thing: read this, then never read anything again.

Before all of this, I was an avid reader of books. If you could find my old bedroom, you'd find piles of books, new and second hand and borrowed. I pondered the power of the brain with Sacks, found my beating heart with Austen and reeled at the unreal reality of Atwood's worlds. You name it, I'd probably read it – or at least had it on my reading list. My family and the few friends I had all warned me. They told me I needed to get out more, to start exploring the flesh and blood of reality instead of clinging to the comfort of paper, ink, e-readers and LCD screens. While they were hunched over their smartphones and social media profiles, I was curled around a book hunting crocodiles and having tea with tigers.

I got a place at university to read English Literature. The other students joined societies and learned the rules of drinking games. I read Chekov, Hardy, Foucault and signed up for the latest updates from the big literary journals. I got through my first year without making any new friends of the flesh and blood sort. Books were all I ever needed.

When the summer came, I went back to Mum's house. Our small, rural town was duller than ever. Being grossly over-active and adventurous is all people do around here. I used to think they were all such fools for choosing raw reality and filtered social media over erudite paper-and-ink books. All I wanted to do over the summer break was read. My summer job at the café didn't last long. Taciturn, vacant, useless were the words used in my exit interview. Mum felt that this was a problem. Her friend suggested I do some volunteer work to socialise me and so this is how this story starts, with Mum signing me up to the Buddy Programme for Disadvantaged Children. They paired up me, a social introvert, with a socially introverted child in the hope that our reluctance to socialise would cancel each other out.

The first day I picked up Helen, I stared deep into her big brown eyes and wondered what the hell I was supposed to do with a seven-year-old who didn't talk. Helen has this weird habit of staring right into your soul like she could whip it out of your chest simply by looking at you. I suppose she didn't like me much at first either. I said 'let's go' and she grabbed my hand without a word and didn't let go until we reached the café. I bought her a hot chocolate and we stared at each other until the mugs were drained. Then I took her home again. The whole time, she didn't say a word. She simply stared her soul-snatching death stare and clutched my hand like she was trying to squeeze the blood out of it.

We followed the same script for a few weeks and I wondered if this was what being social was really like. The more she stared at me, the more I realised she'd been bullied into this too. I felt sorry for her. As an adult, I had the power to say no, I could have escaped our weekly meetings if I'd really tried. She didn't have that option.

One week, I altered our course and took her for a walk through the Memorial Gardens. It was a warm day and there were dog walkers and day drinkers, couples and joggers. People tried to smile at us and Helen would stare her death stare. She had a magical way of repelling everyone. I liked that about her.

We were on our way back towards town and I was thinking about taking her for another hot chocolate when a Frisbee slipped between the trees and cracked her square on the nose. At first, Helen didn't react. She maintained her death stare and didn't blink even when an older couple stopped to ask if she was okay. I knelt beside her and looked deep into the wet glaze on her eyes. *Helen? You alright?*

A young man came crashing through the trees and swore when he saw a small crowd gathering around the small, angry-looking child. A woman shouted at him and he ran over to Helen and tried to apologise. She erupted into an almighty roar. The first real sound I'd ever heard her make. She didn't stop until the crowd dispersed in fear and embarrassment. The young man grabbed his Frisbee and ran off. I picked up Helen and carried her towards the parking lot while wondering how much hearing aids cost. Seven-year-olds are quite heavy, so I had to put her down after a few short streets. Helen stopped screaming and stared at the large grey-white building ahead of us.

'That's the library... have you been before? I go there a lot. But we can only go together if you're quiet,' I told her.

Her death stare said it all. I believe that bookworms are like tapeworms: parasitic creatures that live inside of us. To lure a bookworm out, you have to offer it some literature and wait to see what comes writhing out and I could see Helen had parasitic bookworm potential.

I took her into the library and settled her down on a sunbleached green bean bag in the children's section. I started her off with a bit of classic Jo Cowley and Maurice Gee and before long she was *Juggling with Mandarins* and running from *The Bone Tiki*'s tohunga makutu. I sent her down the rabbit hole, through the looking-glass and even through cupboard doors to button-eyed worlds. We went back week after week and it wasn't long until she was choosing her own books and we could both safely navigate buddy day without social interaction. The only people we'd speak to were the meddling librarians, who kept us hooked up to books new and old like dealers pushing cocaine.

And that's why I'm worried. I think the librarians had something to do with this... it's partly my fault, for bringing Helen to the library. But I didn't know any better. Librarians, the keepers of books – they're the lion tamers of this circus and I'm sure they're aware. They let us read too much and they led us into this trap. They let the bookworms consume us whole.

It was Helen who found the book. An average-looking, dusty hardback with a garish yellow cover. It was the kind of book that had been printed in the 1940s in the style of an 1880s classic. I glanced over to check the title, but it had been lettered in cheap gold embossing and I couldn't make it out. Helen gave me her death stare, so I dove back into *The Cherry Orchard* and entered a doomed household with a broken saucer on the floor.

At the thud of an axe, I glanced up and noticed Helen had gone. There was a warm dent in the bean bag where she'd been sitting and the yellow book was open, lying face down fewer than 20 pages in. I put my finger in as a placeholder and glanced around the library. The sun, the students, the tourists... it was all as normal, but Helen wasn't in sight. I ducked around the nearest bookshelf and dumped the yellow book there. There was a sudden sound – like the string of a viola snapping – and I looked up and saw a man lying on a sofa, neither of which had been there before.

'You've got no strength left,' he said, 'got nothing left, nothing at all. You're just a – nincompoop.'

I felt an uncomfortable, sickly lurch, like a plot twist in my guts. The man lay motionless on the sofa. *Hopefully, he's just a drunk, sleepy tourist*, I thought. *The librarians will wake him up.*

I whispered Helen's name again and again. The library shelves began to melt around me and the sunlight changed hue.

I turned around and found myself in a miserable situation. A group of men stood thoughtfully around a piano. One of them sent for someone's Aunty and a small boy with a book in his hands was crying. Then, there was a loud scraping sound and the scene ran like a watercolour painting left in the rain.

A few more pages passed me by until I realised what was happening.

The thing is, if you land in a well-written book with characters that feel real, it's hard to fathom whether you're in a book or back in the real world. I've been fooled a few times by this – plucking up the courage to ask someone for help, only to find that they can't hear or see me because I'm not in this book. To them, I am not real.

When the ink is sharp and fresh, their voices are clear and crisp. In older books, there's an echo and the edges are yellowy and dim. Mostly, the books smell like half-eaten ham sandwiches. Above me, I can see the edges of the book I'm in, but the ground feels as solid as it always did. Every time I walk to the long edge of a page, there's a scrape and a soft *slap* sound – and I've gone from page 100 to 101. I keep walking. A perpetual dream. A perpetual nightmare.

The feeling of slipping from one page to the next depends on how I'd feel about reading the book. I slid through a collection of short stories by Sarah Hall like a sparrow through the spring rain.

But the 400+ page romance novel felt viscous, like walking through midwinter snow, stumbling in unseen potholes.

At first, I think I was in Fiction, E – H. I was hoping to find Helen in H. But after wading my way through Haddon, Harrison and some lengthy Hardy, I arrived at a mixed shelf. J, P, M, A. I think I'm in Returns. I have to keep going. My theory is that, eventually, I'll come to the end of this bookcase and I'll fall out of the book at the end. I hope I don't have to make my way back to the yellow book... I've forgotten what shelf I left it on and I couldn't bear to walk through all those plots backwards.

Maybe Helen is lost in the children's section? Giving her soul-snatching death-stare to Benjamin Bunny. I hope she's okay. Or maybe she's behind this too. Then I hope she's not okay.

I'm not sure what you can do, or who you can tell. But please, get me out of here somehow. Or, at the very least, put some decent books ahead of me.

THE ARTEFACT PROJECT

SHE WAS mine only for the summer. My sister was going through marital problems, so I agreed to look after the child while they finalised their arguments and began their divorce.

She was six. Maybe seven. Young enough to need constant attention, old enough to cause trouble.

I enrolled her in the local summer school so I could get her out of the way for four hours a day and could focus on my work. I was at a critical point in my artistic career. I'd hit a creative block, a dry spell, for a long while. But finally, I felt I was on the brink of something big. Something good. Besides, I had gone to summer school at about the same age; the other kids bullied me and the teachers turned a blind eye to it – the perpetrators were talented academics and the teachers hoped they'd join the term-time school and boost the school's stats. It was a defining experience for me and I thought a similar experience would toughen up the child, ready for the years ahead of shared custody and awkward door-step goodbyes.

She's from the city. My sister is a hot-shot lawyer. The kind who likes to live in high-rise buildings, all sharp, shiny glass and steel. My sister dresses sharply, acts sharply. Wears expensive watches and sharp, heeled shoes. My town is small and woolly. The silhouettes of the hills are softened by woolly green shrubs and trees, there's a smattering of black-faced, hyphen-eyed sheep in every field and the buildings are all made of stone worn soft with weather and age. The town always smells slightly damp.

They dropped her off in a silver BMW 1 Series that looked like it disliked getting its tyres dirty. I drove her to summer school in my '93 Toyota Corolla that spun mud into the air like a Catherine wheel at every steep corner. One of the summer school teachers greeted her at the green rusted gates, his cheeks were ruddy red and he wore an orange and blue woolly jumper.

'Hello, hello, who do we have here?' – he was much too friendly for my liking.

'This is Sofia... my sister's,' I replied, shoving the child towards him. Sofia. Such a pretentious city name. My sister always has to have her things a cut above. A slice more sophisticated than the rest of us.

'Aha! Hello there, Sofia!' – he spoke like a man on a steamship leaving port. It annoyed me – 'And you! I know you.'

'Yes, you might. I'm an artist.'

'That's right! But your dad, he was an artist too. The one that did that thing with the sheep?'

The sheep. People always bring up my dad and the sheep.

'Yes. I'm actually working on something big myself right now,'

'Better than the sheep? Ho. Ho. Watch out! And you, Sofia? Do you want to be an artist like your granddad?' He pressed his hands into his knees and bent down to look her square in the face. Sofia smiled politely but didn't answer.

'Well, I don't know about your granddad and his sheep, but we stick to crayons and pencils around here. Maybe some acrylics if you're careful. Ho, ho!'

'Behave yourself,' I told her and gripped the handle of my handbag so tightly, I split the edge of my nail on the metal slide adjuster. I sucked the blood and turned back to the rusty gates.

At home, I got to work on my latest commissioned project – a photography series on the remnants of medieval artefacts for the historical society. Wearing cotton gloves, I carefully placed each rusted arrowhead and pottery fragment under the glaring lights in the white box of my studio and photographed its decaying form. I wasn't working on anything better. I was as uninspired as my neglected flower boxes, but I felt buoyant that afternoon. I knew I was on the brink of something big. Something better. I could feel it.

I returned for Sofia at two o'clock and she bounced out of the gates. Mr Orange and Blue Woolly Jumper told me she'd had a great day and the child didn't deny it. She smiled all the way home. I still had two arrowheads and a chamber pot handle to photograph so I sat her down in the corner of the studio on a cushion with two chocolate biscuits, a mug of apple juice and a magazine with lots of pictures in it. She sat quietly until I'd almost finished.

'What are you picturing?'

'Old things, found things,' I told her.

She wandered over to the white box and pulled an old feather and a chewed, slightly muddy biro from her dress pockets. She held her chubby hands out flat, presenting the items for my inspection.

I placed the feather under the lights and photographed it in the same level of detail as the artefacts. I did the same with the biro and talked her through Photoshop as I tweaked the aspect ratio and made sure the edges were sharp and the light was crisp. Transfixed, her eyes followed each jittery movement as the printer churned out a high quality (and expensive) print of the biro and the feather. On impulse, I pinned up some string in the living room and pegged the two prints up on the wall.

'Looks like an art project,' I said, imagining the works in a clinical city art gallery, stripped of their context and bolstered with some jumped-up and obscure *raison d'etre*. It felt like the start of something. Something award-winning.

Sofia looked pleased and I knew then that her being here was good for me.

After she'd gone to bed, my sister called. She was wearing her brisk work voice. It sounded like enquiring after her daughter was a tick-box task, the last on her to-do list before she could open a bottle of wine to drink away the day. I tried to make it sound like Sofia and I were having fun. My only experience of kids was being one, so I'd resolved to treat her like an equal, but with extra offerings of juice and biscuits. But I wanted my sister to think I had everything under control, that there was nothing she needed to worry about – that I could handle a child as easily as a hot-shot lawyer could.

'I photographed some trinkets she brought home, it's actually given me this really great idea for an art piece,' I babbled.

I heard my sister suck air through her teeth then sigh in an odd sort of way, like something she'd learned from a meditation app.

'Look. I didn't want to say anything before because it's really not that much of a problem, but I want you to watch out for that,' she said.

'For what?'

'Her bringing back things. She goes through phases and my lord you can imagine how embarrassing that is for a lawyer. I brought her up to be honest...'

'She borrows things?'

'Well, she doesn't always return them is the issue here.'

'She's a klepto?'

'Look, she's too young to put labels on... just watch for it, will you? I have enough problems without her developing nasty little habits out in the country.'

I mimicked my sister's teeth-suck-and-sigh breathing and assured her it was not a problem and it would not be a problem.

The next afternoon, Sofia brought me a bootlace. Mr Orange and Blue Woolly Jumper watched her skip happily out of the gate and into the Corolla. I searched her red and happy face and asked her how her day was and she held out the bootlace in reply. It was black and muddy like a lake-bottom eel and worn at each end where it'd been tied and retied.

'Okay,' I told her, 'Looks like something else for our art project, hey?'

I drove us home and sat her on the cushion in the corner of my studio with biscuits and a mug of juice, but she insisted on staying right beside me, bubbly snots popping and retracting in and out of her nose as she breathed down my neck.

'Fine. But the biscuits and juice stay in the corner – this stuff's expensive, okay?'

She acquiesced and followed me about, breathing noisily. When we'd finished, I locked the door to my studio and pulled on the round handle twice; the door resisted in a reassuring way. I pegged the photograph of the bootlace on the wall – we'd opted for the image where the bootlace was coiled in a lazy s-shape. It was a nice contrast to the chewed biro and the feather.

The day after, she brought me a button. It was muddy too (all the things she brought me that summer were), and the mud was ingrained into the recesses of the button's floral art nouveau design. The historical society emailed that day to say they were happy with the artefact photographs and I emailed back asking if I could include some of the images in a new art piece I was working on. It would be an exhibition of artefacts: old and new, I told them. The curator wrote back to me with words of encouragement and the contact details of a 'friend-of-a-friend', an art dealer who may be interested. I knew then, that this was it.

This was the start of my big thing.

By the end of the fortnight, I'd pinned another piece of string to the wall and pegged up images of the coat button, the biro, the bootlace, a receipt for two coffees dated six months ago, a moulded torn photograph showing only sepia legs in jeans and corduroy. On the opposite side of the living room, I'd pinned up the photographs I'd taken for the historical society; the arrowheads, pottery fragments and a buckle worn and rusted almost beyond recognition.

I was due to start a new client job, photographing pricey leather purses with floral designs. It was a well-paid job, but the purses remained in the box they'd been couriered in. I spent my days re-arranging the pictures on the walls, thinking about my art exhibition. Sofia brought me a pearlized shirt button and a navy-blue sock with mauve spots on it, worn at the heel and damp to the touch. The next day she brought me a floral Kath Kidston purse: well-loved, muddy, empty. The items felt like they belonged together and it was rewarding to place photographs of the fragments side-by-side. There was a completeness to the action, like something solved.

One damp afternoon Sofia leapt into the Corolla and presented me with a crucifix. It was small and delicate, with tiny brown stones, perhaps Tiger's Eye, at each point. The silver chain and cross was tarnished with rusty-coloured dirt but it didn't look like it had been lying around for a long time. It looked like something recently loved.

I asked Sofia where she found these things, but she only smiled and shrugged.

'They're old things, found things,' she said.

'You're definitely finding them? Nobody is missing this, are they?'

'Nope.'

I asked Mr Orange and Blue Woolly Jumper but he misplaced my concern, I think, and simply assured me that he made her wash her hands before eating lunch. He said Sofia was a shy child who didn't talk much. She preferred to play in the grounds by herself than take part in group activities. He had no complaints, she seemed happy, he said, *ho, ho.*

The day after, a prestigious art gallery in the city called to say there would be a three-month exhibition of my work. They even sent an advance and were already hammering out a campaign on social media. I called to tell my sister, who only wanted to talk about her soon-to-be ex-husband. She'd almost forgotten Sofia, except as a paper pawn in the divorce proceedings. I felt a flash of pride: I was doing a much better job of looking after the child than my sister would have been and it was easier than I'd expected it to be. The artefact project had given us something to conspire on together.

I told the art gallery that I had all of the pictures I needed, that I'd already selected the final images for the exhibition, but Sofia kept bringing artefacts home, right up until the last day of summer school. There was a simple, tortoise-shell hair clasp, with a clutch of auburn hair trapped in the rusted metal clips. A pair of sunglasses, one lens missing, the other scratched and broken and splatted with... mud or something thicker, that had dried into dark stains.

On the last day of summer school, I left the engine of my '93 Toyota Corolla running, exhaust fumes sending clouds into the chilled, almost-autumn air. I ran to the green rusted gates with a customary thank-you note and a box of chocolates for the teacher, but Mr Orange and Blue Woolly Jumper was not there. The primary school teacher who was standing in for him told me he'd had to leave early, he'd gone to the city on a course – or 'something like that,' but the school would pass on the thank-you and chocolates.

I told Sofia we'd be going to the city that afternoon. My sister had full custody and wanted her back. The art gallery wanted the prints.

'I have one more art-ee-fact,' she said, emphasising the word in all the wrong places. She smiled.

In the studio, she pulled a finger out of her pocket and held it flat on the palm of her hand. It was blue and purple and slimy. Some of the skin had come off in her pocket and a thin shard of bone glistened at the very end. My own fingers hovered over the severed finger. I sucked air through my teeth, then sighed. Sofia smiled broadly and looked up at me without tilting her head.

'This is the start of something,' she said.

I put on some cotton gloves, picked up this most delicate of artefacts and placed it carefully into the white box. The shutter noise shot through the air and the computer hummed quietly while Sofia waited by the printer.

As afternoon slipped into a dark and cloudless evening, my car shook as it warmed up into fifth gear on the open road towards the city. The town's damp smell faded behind us. Sofia swung her legs, careful not to let her muddied shoes hit the front passenger seat.

'So, did you have a good summer?'

She smiled, traced lines on the palm of her hand and lifted her eyes to meet mine in the rear mirror.

A Good Dog

ONE MORNING IN EARLY SPRING, Father came home with a new puppy. Just a month old, she was all hair and teeth with a whispy tail protruding from a skinny, young body. Boy went through the typical cycle of emotion when a new creature is introduced into a happy household. On the first day, Boy was thrilled. He showed Puppy every room of the house. Showed her where Mother kept the snacks and showed her all the interesting corners of the garden.

Beyond Mother's carefully-attended garden of hydrangeas and climbing roses was a section of dry earth and weak grass. Father had once kept it neat and tidy with lush, green grass, but successive hot summers and watering bans made the task difficult and besides, Boy loved to race around on the hard, dry earth. Boy showed Puppy the patchy patch of grass. He showed her how to race around and around and how to roll and skid and jump. When they were having too much fun to return to the house, Boy showed Puppy where she could pee in the bushes, a spot that Mother wouldn't find, under the cool shade of a stunted conifer.

A few very happy afternoons passed. Every morning, Puppy was still there and Boy began to wonder when Father would take

Puppy back to her home. But Puppy stayed. Part of the family, a
new responsibility, Mother said. Puppy got toys and baskets and a
new collar. Puppy got cuddles and treats and taken to training
sessions and called a 'Good Girl' for doing the simplest of tasks like
sitting and lying down. If Boy begged for treats he was being a
nuisance, if Puppy begged for treats she was an *adorable, Good
Girl!* When they went for a walk on the beach, Puppy would be
carried in Mother's arms because she hadn't had her immunisa-
tions yet. Boy did not remember being carried in Mother's arms.
Boy tried to run and leap and roll in the sand but Puppy would
wriggle and yelp and want to join him so Mother told Boy to stay
close, so as not to over-excite Puppy.

When summer squeezed the home with relentless heat and
drought, the patchy patch of grass became drier and Father said
Boy wasn't to play on it. There were water restrictions in place and
it was too hot to walk on the sandy beach, too hot to do anything.
On one particularly lethargic Sunday, Boy lay on the carpet in the
living room, looking at the sea whose waves winked at him in the
sun. Mother lounged on an armchair, her book lying open, pages-
down on the arm of the chair and she played with a delicate silk
and wood fan, decorated with roses. Father stood listlessly at the
centre of the living room, socks off and beige 'weekend' trousers
rolled up to his midshins. Puppy raced around the living room.
She was still all fur and teeth and her whispy tail beat at the thick,
summer air. When no one moved, she whipped up the room by
snapping at the fan and pulling at the beige trousers. Boy rolled
over to see Mother's and Father's reactions. They smiled. They
laughed. They rubbed her belly and asked her to do tricks. Father
went to the pantry for pieces of dried veal, he kneeled on the floor
and asked for Puppy's paw, giving her a treat and ruffling the soft,
thin fur on her head when she did as he asked.

He got up and sat beside Puppy. He wanted a treat too. His
mouth salivated and he patiently begged for a treat. Mother and
Father ignored him. So, when Puppy rolled, Boy rolled. When

Puppy shook paws, Boy copied. But he still didn't get any treats. Puppy excitedly span around and around the room, snapping at dust suspended in the sunlight. Mother and Father laughed.

'Look!' They cried. 'Isn't she adorable?'

They looked at Boy and Boy glowered back. He could feel a sickness running through his veins. The more Puppy span, the more he felt sick. Then, suddenly, Puppy lost control and skidded into him. She was almost weightless, all skin and bone and fur and that whispy, wagging tail whipped his face. Boy leapt on her and sunk his teeth into that stupid tail and Mother and Father screamed in two different pitches. Puppy whimpered and cried in a pitch that sat snugly between theirs. Mother gathered Puppy into her arms and Father grabbed Boy and marched him to the spare bedroom.

'Stay!' he yelled.

Boy cried at the door for half an hour and when his whimpering wore thin, he lay by the gap beneath the door and listened. He inhaled the smell of the carpet. It smelt newer than the rest of the house, less trampled, and he let its fibres tickle his nose.

Eventually, Father let him out and led him to the living room and sat him in front of Puppy.

'I want you two to be the best of friends.'

Puppy rolled onto her back and her tongue lolled about her mouth. Boy turned his nose up at her and looked at Mother, then Father. Puppy's eyes glistened, and the white rim of her eyeballs made her look slightly alarmed. Boy sighed and lay down on the carpet beside Puppy, who yelped in delight and licked his neck and ears. They spent the rest of the evening on the carpet, rolling around each other and playing. *Now, isn't that lovely?* Mother said to herself. Boy noticed the softness in Mother's eyes as she watched them play together. He noticed that when he played with Puppy, she looked on them both with the same eyes.

Summer reached its climax. The sun was harsh and the days were long and tiring. The hydrangeas turned brown and stopped flowering and the roses hung their heavy heads. Mother lounged in her armchair with her book and Father tinkered in the shade of the garage. But Puppy and Boy didn't miss an opportunity to play together. Boy began to love Puppy and Puppy loved Boy.

While Mother sat with her book on the armchair and Father tinkered in the garage, Puppy and Boy snuck down to the patch of grass at the bottom of the garden. They'd race around and pee under the bushes and roll in the dried earth until Father spotted them and told them off for wearing down the worn-out grass. So they'd beg to go to the beach. By then, Puppy was allowed to run free so Boy showed her the seaside essentials: how to snap at the waves and chase the seagulls (though they never managed to catch one). He taught her how to chase the waves and together they'd leap with excitement as the waves rolled over them, washing their skin with salt. Mother and Father would stand in the sea, cooling their feet and gazing out towards a thin line that marked the boundary between sea and sky.

As quickly as admiration for this troublesome twosome had bloomed in Mother's and Father's eyes, it faded. Mother borrowed bigger, heavier books from the library. Books that smelled different to her usual paperbacks that sat snugly in one lazy hand. Father made anxious phone calls and shouted a lot. At night, Boy could hear them whispering in harsh tones and in the morning their whispered nights would hang in heavy half-moons under their eyes.

When late autumn brought with it inconsistent rain and a cooling breeze, the patchy patch of grass transformed into a shallow mud pool with thin spears of revived grass. Boy and Puppy would roll in whatever mud they could find. Weeks before, they'd stopped going to the beach but Puppy and Boy could still smell the salt of the sea on the air and he'd tell Puppy that one day, they'd snap at the sea and chase the gulls again. Fat, slightly sour apples plummeted from their neighbour's tree into the edge of the garden and the brown hydrangeas folded in half like they'd given up. Puppy was larger now, beginning to grow out of her Puppy-ish-ness. Boy had grown over the summer too. When they played rough-and-tumble in the living room, chairs would be knocked over and lamps would topple and Father would drag Boy to the spare room and Puppy to the outhouse. Boy would lie at the door and smell the carpet and cry and yelp. Puppy would call back, each voice getting louder and louder until Father would start shouting and neighbours would complain and neither Puppy nor Boy would get supper. In the morning, Boy would try to do the tricks – roll, shake, sit, lie and Puppy would dutifully copy him but Father would sniff and thump his hand on the table and Mother would quietly cry.

Winter was in the air on the day that Puppy and Boy knocked over the coat stand. They eyed Father as he picked up the stand and their ears twitched at the sound of Mother sobbing in the next room. This time, there was no shouting. No being pulled into separate rooms and no howling into the carpet of the spare room. Puppy shuffled backwards so that she was behind Boy and Boy stood firm. Father rearranged the coats on the coat stand and sniffed once. Boy looked at Puppy, a wildness in his eyes, and bolted for the back door. Puppy followed him through the garden to their favourite patch and they tore around the ruined grass snapping at wayward fallen leaves and barking at blackbirds who rose themselves into the skies with a quick pulse of their wings. Freedom pulsed through their veins and clung to the dew on the branches of dead roses. Freedom was in the mud that was flung into the air as they chased each other around and around the patchy patch of grass. Freedom was in the way that Puppy always submitted to Boy, the way her eyes followed his thoughts and the way that her trust lay in his lap.

They stopped trying to catch the leaves so that they could catch their breath, and they lay on their backs in the mud and sighed.

Puppy's ears twitched as she heard the latch of the front door click.

She sat up and looked at Boy who rolled over and sat up too.

Dutifully, Puppy waited until Boy leapt up and started to run, then Puppy gave chase. They tore around the patch once, twice, then scarpered up to the door where they landed in a pile on the doorstep yelping and barking and puffing with excitement. Then, when the smell of salt and grass and excitement subsided, they noticed the strange men standing at the door, looking at them both. Mother was crying and Father was holding her.

'He was such a good Boy, such a good Boy.'

The men nodded to each other and tried to coax Boy towards a van that was parked in the driveway. Puppy instinctively growled and Boy copied, snapping at them and drawing himself to full height. Dead grass clung to his bruised knees and he staggered as he re-adjusted his weight over his hips and feet. The men paused for a moment, wary of Boy's wild, wolfish looks. Then they lurched towards him and grabbed his arms. They pulled him towards the van, at first gently, but then more roughly as Boy struggled and barked and snapped at them. As they pushed him into the back of the van Puppy cried and yelped and didn't stay still for a second. Father grabbed Puppy and attached a rope to her collar. Mother looked at Boy in the back of the van.

'Oh, my son was such a good Boy, such a good Boy, once,' she sobbed.

Father sniffed sharply and turned his gaze towards a lone dandelion struggling between paving stones, then looked at Mother.

'I think it's best we get rid of the dog, too.'

THE RUNNER

TEDDY SITS FOUR FEET AWAY, half perched on the end of a truck. He's eating brown bread tuna sandwiches and looking intently at his boots in the sunshine. A few small birds greedily hop near his feet. Inquisitively rocking their heads this way and that, sussing out the trajectory of loose bread crumbs.

Joel stares at Teddy. Teddy's admiring the way that the sun-deprived tongues of his shoes are a darker shade than the uppers. He's thinking about laying carpets, because even though Teddy has been a carpet-layer since the age of sixteen, he doesn't get bored of laying carpets, not really.

'Every carpet is different, every room is different,' Teddy often says.

'Not quite like snowflakes – but it isn't my job to lay the snowflakes, eh?'

Teddy is married. He's mentioned it before. His wife Emily is the ambitious type who somehow also managed to be the ambi-tion-fulfilling type. She used to go on business trips to London a lot, a sure sign of any successful business person. Teddy thinks about her often. 'Emily'll like those,' he'd say, wrenching daffodils, roots and all, from an untended berm near the new housing development. Since starting the job, Joel has gravitated towards Teddy. He's like a planet, thinks Joel; Teddy is strong, centred, confident in his time and space in the universe. The lads on the building site revolve around him like satellites.

Joel shifts from the shadows and creeps towards Teddy.

Teddy looks up.

'Allgood?'

'Aye.'

A pause. Teddy's not sure what to ask now he has established Joel is *allgood*.

'Shame to be toiling when the sun's shining, eh?'

'Aye.'

'Goodday to be outside. Are you running them races again? You used to be in the papers, didn't you? Running them hills. I remember. Used to be a bit of a runner myself, back then.'

The running. That feeling of whole-body connectedness. Every tendon, ligament, every scrap of muscle, blood and bone and hormones all working in harmony. The tightness in his calves and buttocks as he pushed himself up rough and rugged mountains. The sweet taste of iron under his tongue. The cool metal of trophies and medals. The warm flush of ego, of feeling known, looked up to, honoured for his talent.

'Nah. Not so much.'

'Time getting away with you, eh? I'm tired of laying carpets, time's getting on to retire. Lay myself down somewhere sunny and have myself a beer.'

Joel blinks. He wants to ask about Teddy's wife and Teddy's contentedness. How it feels to be *the* Teddy Harrison. At night, Joel often pulls the bedsheets over his head, closes his eyes and inhales deeply. Death had taken his Angela long ago, but on his better days, he imagines he can still smell her body close to his in the moments before sleep. Not the Angela that reeked of cancer and spoilt milk. His Angela.

Teddy stops chewing his brown bread tuna sandwich. The

birds cock their heads, wondering what the delay is all about. A fat, red-faced one with yellow wing tips edges forward, considering the possibility of wresting the half-sandwich from Teddy and taking the lot home. On its second assessment, it decides that Teddy and the other birds would probably gang up on it and the likelihood of being crushed in the scuffle is too high. It hops back into place and waits with the others.

'You never come for beers, much, do you? But the young lads from the site can be gobshites. They're jus' young. Don't have the life experience we do, hey? But you should come over ours for Easter. Emily makes an egg hunt that keeps the grandkids busy and we have a few beers around the BBQ. A bit more relaxed than the nights out with the lads from the site. You'd like it. I'll write down the address for you later, yeah?'

'Aye... ta, Teddy.'

'Lovely. But we should probably get back to it, eh? Lots to be done. No rest and all that malarkey.'

Teddy throws the remainders of his brown bread tuna sandwich to the ground and a small-scale scuffle takes place between the birds. Teddy pats Joel on the shoulder once and walks back towards the house they're working on.

Joel stands still, head hung low, and watches the birds. They scrap viciously and noisily. He thinks about how there's nothing cute or idyllic about wildlife. He thinks about how they're fighting to live, that their every moment is focused on survival. He thinks about how he does not have that kind of focus. He knows there's no fight left in him.

A nestling stands on the periphery of the group, oversized pink legs folded beneath it, yellow mouth downturned. The baby bird shivers in its unformed feathers and drapes one hairy wing behind itself. As Joel kneels to inspect it, the other birds recede and then come crashing back in a wave. Recede and crash. Recede and crash. Afraid of his presence, but overcome by desire for a brown bread tuna sandwich. The baby bird doesn't flinch. Joel can see flies buzzing around it and maggots crawling over the bare pink flesh near where its tail feathers should be.

Two young labourers stand on the porch of the house. They start a loud conversation half-directed at him about lazy old men slowing the team down.

Joel hoists himself up. Knees feeling dry and concrete-cold. The birds flutter again, coming in waves. He shuffles over to the nestling. The baby bird lowers its eyelids but doesn't flinch as Joel brings his heavy work boot down onto it. He feels nothing underfoot, so he twists his toes in the dirt to make sure he's cleanly killed it. He doesn't check.

Joel pulls an uneaten ham bun from his pocket and tosses it to the birds.

It's evening. The thin, single-pane glass shudders as Joel roughly kicks the front door shut. Joel doesn't lock the door. He hasn't locked any doors since Death took Angela. He knows no lock can keep fate at bay. Death has no respect for keys and locks.

Joel kicks his boots into the corner by the door and wanders slowly to the kitchen, a bare toe protruding from his faded black socks leading the way.

He wonders if he is hungry. He's not sure how long he wandered the streets for. For a while, after Death took Angela, Joel tried learning the piano. He took up woodwork and toyed with origami. But nothing could fill the hole he felt in his soul and meeting other people was out of the question – he couldn't let Death have them too.

In the fridge, there's a can of coke, an empty sliced ham wrapper and a tub of luminous yellow margarine pock-marked with crumbs of burnt toast. He inspects the grease on the inside of the ham wrapper, then pops it in the pedal bin by the door.

He takes the coke and watches the fizz bounce out of the can as he opens it. He can smell the sugar and caffeine and all the numbers of a chemical rainbow. He takes a sip, pursing his mouth like a salmon as he does so.

Joel lives in an orange house. The living room is orange and is attached to the hallway, which is attached to the kitchen. The orange paint spreads across all of the walls. The wooden floor, cupboards doors and shelves and the kitchen table are all cheap pine tainted with cheap orangey varnish. It's smooth and shiny with any possible rustic edges sanded away.

The other rooms are faded white. It's a two-bedroom, one-bathroom downstairs affair. It's sparsely furnished with things that don't fit in elsewhere in the house and clothes he'll never wear. In the garage, there's a pile of cardboard boxes that have remained unpacked for so long, Joel doesn't remember what's in them anymore.

It was such a long time ago when they left Newcastle. When he gave up running. When he thought all it would take to break the curse was to pretend he was someone else, pretend he wasn't the world-famous runner, who could move so fast he could literally outrun Death.

They had once thought they could be happy here.

No. Wait. He thought they could live happily here. Angela never wanted to leave Newcastle. She warned him moving South and giving up running wasn't enough. That Death knew no boundaries. That Death would still come for him.

A devil's coach-horse beetle skitters across the floor and disappears between two orange-varnished floorboards.

'Fuck,' says Joel, and stands up. The floral kitchen clock ticks more slowly. It's almost imperceptible, but Joel recognises it as a sign she's coming.

'Fuck ye,' he yells and looks around the kitchen for smoke and shadows.

'Ah'm fucken done. Ye can stop yer nonsense and yer can come get me now. What did ah do? What did ah ever fucken dee to ye?'

There's a flash of light in Joel's mind. He sees his own hand, much younger, reaching for Angela's. Devil's coach-horses crawl over their school shoes. He begins to run and Angela moves with him. They're in the Rising Sun Country Park and the woodland is familiar to them. The landscape blurs and they move so fast, him laughing, Angela making frightened gasps for air. Joel feels the warm flush of his ego spreading throughout his body, the thrill of escaping, his pride in his ability to see Death coming and to run from it, to dodge it like a simple game of catch-and-kiss.

Joel had always known when to run, how to evade Death. It was intuitive, unlearned, like a child's urge to stand after mastering the art of crawling. But it was Angela, his Angela, who'd been the first to come with him, hand-in-hand.

They'd whisked family and friends from Death's grip and together, lived beyond their natural years. It had been Angela, his Angela, who'd had the idea for him to pose as an ultrarunner, carrying souls with him until Death was called away to fulfil her duties elsewhere. The run at Rising Sun was only the first.

'Angie, it's fine. Yer with me, just hold on!' Joel hears his young voice saying, 'Ah cannae believe it, we're deeing it! We're oot-running tha' auld bitch taegether.'

As Joel's mind settles on the pit-house, he can smell the damp soil and dried piss. He sees the two of them huddle in the dark together, Joel holding Angela's inhaler to her mouth and rubbing her back in a circular motion.

'It's allreet, yer alright,' he says again and again and again, 'it's allreet, yer alright. Ah've got ye, Angie. We'll run taegether.

We'll aalways run taegether. Ah've got ye. It's allreet, yer alright.'

And then, the memory stops. He sees and smells his own kitchen again and Angela, the pit-house and the smell of damp earth and piss is gone. A small group of devil's coach-horses patter across the tiles and under the back door, into his unkempt back garden.

'Fuck ye,' he whispers and wrenches open the back door.

'Hadaway ow'er here. Stop hidin' yer slippery bitch! Ah'm ready for ye!'

But there's nothing in the dark garden, but bushes shivering in an agitated breeze. Joel thinks he sees two red orbs appear in the bushes in the back left of the garden and so he pulls at the grass and bushes in his path, bashing his way awkwardly to that corner. On the fence, a young blackbird calls to him.

Joel looks at the bird and it leaps towards him, landing on a branch a foot from his face. It's young. Still brown and speckled. But its feathers are well developed and he looks strong and proud. The corners of his mouth are slightly yellow and downturned, and as he cocks his head towards Joel, he seems to be frowning, like a teacher disappointed in a student who's progressing more slowly than they should.

Joel reaches out instinctively towards the bird. He wants to feel its feathers, its beating heart and look into its wet, bright eyes. But the bird calls out and bounces to a lower branch where Joel sees the red orbs again.

'Oh, fuck me,' he says, looking at the skeletal creature that's crawling with devil's coach-horse beetles. Satisfied, the blackbird quietly retreats into the dark undergrowth. Joel grabs the creature and tries to brush some of the insects off it. He takes it to the bathroom and showers it, rubbing his orange miner's soap into its skin and hosing off grime and filth and insects. And then he stands back and looks at it.

A skeletal whippet with silky, smoky-coloured fur looks back at him. Her big black eyes don't blink and her tail is looped up between her legs.

'Aren't ye a bonnie lass,' says Joel, rubbing his fingertips into his chest and massaging the hole where his soul should be.

Teddy waves eagerly at Joel.

'Over here, mate! Come round the back.'

Joel tugs at the shoulders of his tee-shirt, thinking it'll make his physique look sharper. He glances down at Bonnie, who wags her tail reassuringly. Together, they walk past the wheelie bins and through the low wooden gate to meet Teddy, Emily, and a couple he assumes to be Emily's friends. They're dressed in casual clothes, but there's a freshness, a subtleness of hue, the gentle way the tee-shirt hugs the woman's breasts that suggests their clothes are expensive. Emily is dressed like them; fitted navy linen trousers, a deep pink jumper with a white piped collar framing her heart-shaped face. Joel thinks she looks lovely and is embarrassed.

'Joel! Great. Great you're here,' beams Teddy.

He's wearing beige trousers, a beige floppy hat and a maroon tee-shirt with a stain down the front. A smile breaks across Joel's face. Unused to facial expressions, his skin feels like old plaster.

Two children scream and run the length of the large garden with a lime green plastic toy in hand. Bonnie yelps and runs after them, brushing past Joel as she leaves his side, where she's most often found since his appearance in Joel's garden six months ago. His eyes snag on the children for a moment, but he wafts away the feeling that rises in him before it can take hold.

'Well, that's the grandkids of all species entertained,' laughs Teddy, as they watch Bonnie join in the children's game seamlessly. 'I tell you, you're a changed man since you got that dog. Nothing like a dog to take care of to breathe a bit of life back into an old soul... except grandkids, of course,' Teddy picks up a tennis ball that's sitting beside the BBQ and throws it in the direction of the throng. There are more screams and barks of delight. Joel smiles and shakes his head.

'Aye,' he says, and turns to greet Emily and the couple.

There are brief introductions, but the couple seems eager to have Emily to themselves. Emily's eye catches for a moment on the stain on Teddy's tee-shirt. Her lips part and her eyes move to Teddy's face. Teddy is talking animatedly to Joel again. She rolls her eyes at Joel and pats him on the shoulder; 'Well, it's nice to have you over again,' she says, and allows herself to be swept away by the couple and others who come and go for most of the evening.

Teddy and Emily's tired-looking son appears briefly to collect the children. He shakes Joel's hand roughly and leaves quickly. Bonnie resumes her position at Joel's side, looking up at him with white rims showing at the corners of her eyes and Joel hurts his shoulder scratching her ear for too long.

Joel doesn't say much at the barbeque. But he doesn't need to. First, Teddy complains about work, carefully berating everyone and insulting no one. Then, he asks Joel's advice on barbequing sausages and without waiting for an answer, tells Joel a long story about his father's approach to the perfect barbecue.

'It's all in the right coal, the temperature... and of course, having the right tools. You'll be learning something here, Joel. You Geordie lot aren't known for your barbeques are you?'

'Nah, not s'much.'

'You don't get the weather, I suppose. What do youse eat?'

'Ham n' pease pudding... in an eight-inch stottie cake,' grins Joel.

'I'm not one for sweet stuff myself,' says Teddy and Joel doesn't correct him. He likes the cadence of Teddy's voice. He likes that Teddy does the talking.

Even though it's dark, Joel insists on walking home alone. Emily and Teddy take it in turns to tempt him otherwise: she'll make up the spare bed, he'll sort him a taxi. But Joel tells them he likes the fresh air. Quietly, he knows he needs the space to think, to take in all the colours and energy of the evening.

'You used to do all those running races, didn't you? That's you right? Those crazy ultramarathons and that. I suppose there's something about the fresh air and getting places on your own two feet.'

'Emily, I told you it was him. He doesn't want bothered with that now...'

'It's fine,' says Joel, 'Cheers for a really lovely evening, like. Ah've had a deed canny time. But ah'd like to walk meesel yhem.'

Emily kisses him on the cheek and Teddy gives him a big bear hug. Joel feels a rush of warmth in his soul, then a stab of panic. He walks to the front gate, then listens carefully. He can hear Emily and Teddy bickering and laughing. They're okay. Joel looks into the night and it's starlit. The moon hangs heavy in the sky and the air feels warm.

Bonnie looks up at him with her large eyes like orbs. She wags her tail slowly. He begins to run.

It's been a long time since he's ran, really ran, with joy pulsing through his veins and spring-loading the balls of his feet. Bonnie leaps at his side, snapping at his heels, running ahead, then waiting behind. She likes this game.

It's early afternoon on a workday. Joel pulls open his front door and Bonnie shoots at his chest, winding him and causing him to step backwards. He drops his bag to the floor and gathers up the writhing skeletal dog.

'Whoa, Bonnie. Whoa! Aye, I'm home. What of it?'

She wags her tail with almost enough propulsion to take off and nuzzles into his face leaving damp patches and muddy paw prints across his pale-coloured tee shirt. Joel sees that the back door is open and the blackbird is singing from the fence and looking right into his kitchen as if he's checking the time on the clock. He's larger now, with glossy, deep black feathers and a strong voice. Joel's seen a soft brown female scurrying between the bushes and wonders if there'll be a family soon.

Bonnie wriggles in his arms as he pushes his boots off with his toes and roughly kicks them into the smart line of running shoes and soft suede loafers.

He dumps her in the hallway and she continues her energetic parade, following him into the kitchen where he fills her food and water bowl. For a moment, she's too excited by his presence to eat, but being an intelligent dog she soon gathers that there's something wrong with him tonight and she dives into the food.

Joel thinks about Teddy. He thinks about the way his chest was heaving up and down and up and down and up while he was having a heart attack that afternoon. He thinks about the devil's coach-horse beetles looking so out of place in the new build house with its fresh, white walls. There didn't seem to be much fuss. The heart attack was simple and quiet.

Joel had been sitting in an airing cupboard, pretending to finish laying a tricky piece of carpet. He was inspecting the rough, scratched surface of his hands and running a finger along the sharp edge of the knife. He'd felt himself slip into a black hole that emanated from the back of the cupboard. The hole where his soul should be ached and a devil's coach-horse crawled over his face.

The quiet thud of Teddy's carpet knife slipping to the floor hurled Joel back into real time. Teddy would never stop until the job was done, Teddy would never throw tools on the floor. Death was here, and she was here for Teddy.

Joel found Teddy half slumped in the hallway having a heart attack. He remembers reaching for Teddy's hand, saying 'Come with me, mate, we need to move,' but Teddy shook his head.

'Your hands, Joel, you're... so cold. Why is everything so cold?'.

There was an awkward sixteen minutes until the ambulance turned up. Joel remembers the time ticking by slightly slower than it should have. Joel had watched them wheel Teddy into the ambulance and speed off with lights and noise. He went home without talking to anyone, with Angela pulling on the stings of his memories.

'Ah can dee nae right,' Joel says to Bonnie, massaging his

fingers into his chest where he feels the deep hole where his soul could be opening up again.

He sits with his legs spread out on the floor and plays with Bonnie. He thinks about taking her for a run, but he has a headache and tears fall like a fever-driven sweat from his eyes. So he bounces a tennis ball on the floor and watches her slip on the varnish in the scramble to catch it.

She's agile, she's fast. All four paws are in the air, her nose is pointed towards the ball and in a whip-snap she has it, and returns it to him. Tongue out, expressive eyebrows raised in readiness.

I'm ready, I'm ready, I'm ready.

She's thinking only in the present because that's how dogs think. There's only the ball, Joel and her. No memories, no regrets, no Death's curse.

Joel wakes with a jerk. It's late at night creeping into early morning. He's on the floor, the tennis ball squeezed in his tight grip. Bonnie's asleep next to him, leaning her body against his. As he sits up she looks up at him through her eyebrows. She looks stern but wags her tail a little.

'Did I fall asleep Bonnie?'

She sits up too and continues to look at him. She looks stern for one more moment before melting and putting both paws on his legs.

Go to bed.

'Ah'm sorry Bonnie. Ah didn't even walk you did ah? Did ah even feed yer?'

Go to bed.

Bonnies gets up and walks with her tail between her legs towards the bedroom. Her claws tap-tap-tap on the wooden floor. She walks lazily, with a heavy sway in her shoulders that makes her head bob from side to side like a hard-working shire horse pulling a heavy load.

She pauses at the door and looks back at him. He's still sitting on the floor. He stares at the floral clock which is ticking quietly, slowly, on the kitchen wall. It's only nine o'clock but he's so tired.

So tired. He's not sure how long he has been on the floor.

Then, shock takes his body. A sick feeling rises in his throat. She's there. The floral clock ticking a different beat above her right shoulder, the frayed edges of her navy cloak spreading like oil across the kitchen's battered floorboards. Her edges are soft at first, she's just whisps of shadows and smoke but the smoke gathers and builds and her shape grows stronger.

As she becomes more solid and defined, Joel feels the icy touch of thousands of devil's coach-horse beetles crawling across and under his skin. Some of them are shadow creatures, walking in and out of his flesh as if he's barely there. Others are more solid, of this world, and he feels their feet and antennae race across the surface of his skin.

Just like last time, he can't move. Just like last time, he feels his heart stop and his soul snap from his body. The vibration's different in this state. He's more aware of every tiny foot and antennae on his earth-bound body. He can hear the blackbird calling in the neglected garden. The world is refreshingly ice-cold and Death appears before him in startling clarity.

'Joel,' she says, curtly.

'Ah... ah didn't mean tae.'

'Didn't mean to do what, Joel?'

'Make friends. Wi' Teddy.'

'And Emily?'

'Oh, fuck. Ye didn't kill her an' all, did ye?' Death's laugh is soft and warm.

'You've been quite the social creature lately, Joel,'

'Ah didn't dae anything wrang. Ah didn't run, ah didn't help him escape. I stayed right where ah was, an' ah just stayed with him.

Ye knaa ah've not ran from ye since... since...'

Joel can't close his eyes. He can't move. But a familiar smell washes through his body. It's her smell. His Angela's perfume. For a brief moment, he's back there. In his thirties, running, winning races, spending long summer evenings with Angela before all of this... before Death, before endless life, endless death.

'It's ye. Yer wearin' Angela's perfume aren't ye?'

'She had excellent taste, did Angela.'

Joel wants to cry. He wants to beg Death to make it all stop, but he can't. He can't move. Besides, he's tried before. He's begged, he's written letters and burned them in fires, hoping the messages rise to the heavens, or whatever comes next. Death has always refused to answer his questions about the afterlife. She refuses to tell him when his punishment will end. The man who could run so fast, he could outrun Death. The man who refused to surrender his love, his Angela, when Death came for her. Now he runs to her, asking Death for the end only she can grant him.

Joel suddenly becomes aware of two red orbs in the doorway. He can't turn to see them, but he's aware of their presence and hears a click-clack, click-clack of claws on floorboards as the orbs bob closer and closer.

'Is this... is this how I end?' he asks Death.

Death smiles and shakes her head gently. She pulls something small from her pocket and the click-clacking accelerates.

If Joel could inhale sharply, he would.

'Bonnie! Stay, divven't. Gerra way from her!'

The red orbs fade as Bonnie slips into the moonlight pooling in the kitchen and her eyes turn to Death. Death holds a small dog treat in her hand and offers it out to Bonnie.

'Bonnie! Gerra way from her!'

Bonnie dips her head towards the treat like she's curtseying to Death, but then turns away. She looks at Joel's body, then up at Joel's soul.

'Good lass. Stay away from her. She's nae good.'

'Pffft,' spits Death, 'she likes you more than she likes me.'

'An' why would a canny dog like Bonnie like a mean bitch like ye?'

'She's my dog, Joel. She's my familiar,' Death huffs and Joel's mind summersaults, 'I'm here to settle up, Joel. I'm here to start your clock again. I'm tired. I know you're tired and I think we're done here.'

'Wh-what do you mean?'

'The clock is ticking again. You'll die, at some point. I'm not telling you when... but considering you've spent more time with me than the average mortal, I suspect you'll have a sharper idea of how myself and Life works.'

'But... Bonnie? What dya mean Bonnie's yer familiar?'

'Joel. Pay attention. I'm here to tell you I'm releasing you from the curse. You're not immortal anymore and I know you won't try to run off and hide souls from me anymore. We're done here.'

Joel's not paying attention, he focusses his mind on Bonnie, who cocks her head towards his body and slowly wags her tail.

'Oh, for goodness' sake. Is the dog all you care about?' Death looks at Bonnie looking at Joel and Joel focussing all his love on Bonnie. She sees the energy, the vibration between them.

'That's quite cute,' whispers Death. She realises she needs to change tact with Joel, or she'll lose control of the situation.

'Joel. Joel. Hey, listen up. Bonnie *is* one of my many familiars. I sent her down here to keep an eye on you.'

'Bonnie! Bonnie lass... yer a SPY?'

'She's not a spy, Joel. She doesn't report to me. Having an animal connection makes it easier for me to travel here. She's a sweet thing, but we've never really gotten along. I'm more of a cat person, really. Dogs like to run a lot more than I have time for... so I thought... I thought she'd make a nice gift to you, for the remainder of your time here. But you've not really taken her out running as much as I thought you would, so I can take her back home with me if you'd like me to.'

Joel's soul begins to sink back into the hole in his body and the devil's coach-horses skitter away, disappearing into invisible holes in the cupboards and skirting boards. Death begins to fade, her edges softening and becoming wisps of smoke.

Bonnie cries out to Joel. She's becoming smoke too. She whimpers and nuzzles at Joel's body, but he still can't move. Joel panics.

'Don't leave me. Not again. Don't leave me alone. Please.' He watches his thoughts shimmer along vibration lines towards Death. Only Death's face is left now and her smile disappearing into the floral clock is the last thing he sees before he fully re-enters his body and slumps to the floor.

It takes a few seconds for him to grind his cold, sinewy muscles into movement. They feel like wires underneath his skin. They're scraping against the bone and the flesh and they're so taught they're going to snap. He calls, but Bonnie is nowhere to be seen.

He walks towards the floral kitchen clock. On the kitchen bench, there's the tub of margarine looking back at him, telling him it *actively reduces cholesterol.*

Joel lets the quietness of his orange house crowd around him.

He feels like an ocean wave unceremoniously crawling up the sand.

The great drama of deep-sea storms and crashing waves in the past.

He's petering out. A dribble.

He pulls open the knife drawer, but there are only teaspoons and a slightly bent bread knife.

'There was aalways knives when I wanted a bleeding teaspoon,' he mutters.

Joel slams the drawer shut with a clatter, unsure what to do.

He hears the teaspoons jingle in the drawer.

Somewhere, quietly, there's a buzzing sound. Joel follows the sound to one of his old running shoes in the hallway. The buzzing stops then starts up again and his shoe lights up with an eerie, sickly light. Slowly slipping his hand into his shoe, Joel pauses as a devil's coach-horse races up his middle finger, along his arm and drops off his elbow. It disappears between the orange-varnished floorboards.

Joel's fingertips find his mobile phone.

It's Emily calling.

'Joel? Joel... are you there?' she whispers down the line.

'Aye.'

'Oh, Joel. You scared me. I've been trying to call all evening. Teddy insisted I contact you, he knows how you get.'

'Teddy... insisted?'

'Yes. He worries about you, Joel. He cares about you.'

'Teddy?'

'Teddy's fine, Joel. He's just fine. He says it's thanks to you... you insisted on calling the ambulance.'

'Ah did?'

'Yes, Joel. Teddy says he didn't even realise he was having a heart attack. The idiot didn't want to complain about the pain in his chest... have you ever heard of Teddy not complaining? But somehow, somehow you just knew. So I'm calling to say, thank you, Joel. And we'd like you to come around for a barbeque soon... though I think Teddy will be cutting back on the sausages.'

'Ah'd like that, Emily. Jus' when Teddy's feeling up tae it.'

'I'll call you again. Let you know how he's doing.'

Joel looks down at his phone and sees messages from Emily, from the lads at work, from his boss. He walks back to the kitchen, rubbing the spot where his soul could be.

Click-click-click-clack-clack-clack. Two red orbs appear in the doorway behind him.

'Bonnie! Me bonnie lassie! Yer here!'

The smoky grey whippet shoots at his chest and Joel stumbles backwards, knocking the floral kitchen clock to a jaunty angle. He gathers up the writhing, skeletal dog. Her tail wags with powerful propulsion and Joel realises Bonnie always had the option to take off.

'All of this world and the next... and yer chose this sorry auld gadgie.'

She drops to the floor and click-clacks along the hall to the bedroom. Joel looks at her.

'Ah feel so tired, Bonnie lass,' he says.

She stands on the bed until he pulls off all of his clothes apart from his navy coloured boxers and rolls under the sheets. He pulls the old tartan throw closer to him and pats it. Bonnie plonks herself down and edges closer so he can tickle her ears.

'You've got beautiful ears, Bonnie lass.'

She lays her head on her bony legs and looks at him with half-lidded eyes. He lies awake, thinking. He promises himself that he'll go for a morning run with Bonnie.

He rests his hand on his chest and watches the life inside of him rise and fall, rise and fall.

'We'll run te-morrow, Bonnie. Yer'll wake me up? We'll run te-morrow.'

Bonnie thumps her tail against his body. He takes it as a sign of agreement. She's thinking about the steadiness of his heartbeat and his warm hands on her ears. She can hear him talking and he sounds happy and calm. She's happy and calm. Outside, in the dead of night, the blackbird sings.

They fall asleep together.

THE CUCKOO

WE SPOT HER FIRST, from our viewpoint in the top corner of the narrow bathroom, lying in the water which we know went cold hours ago.

She doesn't move. She writhes. And we can see instantly that there is something unnatural about her. The water has an oily quality that clings to her skin each time her lungs push against their cage and break the water's membrane. Her breathing has an irregular pattern, unsustainable by any healthy human being. We see her in a dim candlelight, although we cannot see the light source. Her arm is resting at an awkward angle over the side of the bath and water slides down a finger extended. A stalactite. She could have been there longer. Occasionally, she twists, as one in fire or in lime.

He twists. A key in the lock. A small sound which erupts in a long stagnating silence.

She moves at the sound of his return. Our vision is split between him, at the door of his home, and her, in his bath tub. The door creaks and we're reminded of an old scary film. He stops this happening again via a quick detour to the car for some WD40. He's mildly glad to be home. He leaves his wool coat on the post at bottom of the stairs and shoves his iPhone, the latest model available, into the pocket of his grey suit trousers. He drops a plastic Tesco bag onto the marble kitchen bench. He drinks semi-skimmed milk from the bottle. We're waiting for him to go to the bathroom, but he doesn't. He sits on his leather mid-century sofa in front of his 60-inch smart television for what may be a few hours. We can't tell. A programme about cars and a news programme flash by us. He takes long, gulping drinks from the plastic milk bottle. He watches a comedy show and does not laugh.

All this time, she lies there.

One bottle of semi-skimmed milk, three cups of tea and one beer later, his bladder finally starts to feel flooded. By the time he gets upstairs, he's already unbuttoned, fly down. His hand is in his pants and he's facing the toilet by the time he registers the elongated, grey-skinned woman is in his half-filled bath tub. He lets a steam of profanities bounce against the walls, while she lies very still. He wastes more time standing like that, hand in his pants, mouth slightly open, staring at her. We see her vein-marbled eyes, black pupils slowly dilating, her gaze rolling around to meet his.

He pulls her out of the bath. He has large, strong hands that leave blue prints on her grey flesh. Water spills onto the floor. The thud of her body onto the tiles is an uncomfortable sound. He checks her Airways, Breathing, Circulation. We know, of course, that she's still breathing. We know. But he's confused. He shakes her violently when she responds to each obvious question with an obvious stare. In frustration, he lets her slump onto the floor and gets changed into dry clothes before bringing her a towel and joggers, boxers, that too-small school hoodie. She won't move, so he has to dry and dress her. This is awkward. This takes some time. He notes that every time he touches her, it leaves a blue impression. She shivers and he gives her his dressing gown too. Anything to hide those marks. He sees that she does not have skin, she has flesh and is embarrassed. He gives her socks and a beanie hat.

Our view shifts to the top corner of the living room. We can see the 60-inch smart television. Things move quickly. He creates a makeshift sofa bed using throws, cushions and spare bed sheets but by the time he has finished, she has disappeared. She is nestled in his bed, furled around herself like fern fronds, smiling to herself. As the sickly fluoresce from the street lamp transforms into blocks of rose tinted sunlight, we see his squarish figure lying on the makeshift sofa bed, limbs at angles. His eyes are open. He is not smiling.

The morning light is cool and uniform. We follow him to the dumping room he calls The Study. He's staring at his iPhone, the latest available that does so much more than make phone calls, but he uses it like a Nokia 3310. He's making a phone call; *Hello, police?* He's using Google voice search on his rose-gold tablet; *What should you do when...* He is typing an email; *To Whom It May...* He's sitting alone, pulling at the skin around his eyes, staring at the floor.

When he leaves the study, she is sitting by the door, with her mouth a little open. She follows him to the kitchen, where the innards of the cupboards resemble Andy Warhol prints. He opens two cans of soup, pours them into matching striped bowls and heats them in the microwave.

As the time ticks down on the microwave's lime green clock, our vision blurs and settles on a new scene. We see him, but much younger. Wearing worse clothes, unironed, unconcerned. We see him attempt to put the key into a black-painted wooden door. It is a navy sky that hangs above him, and a petite red haired girl that hangs on his arm. He attempts to put the key in the lock again. She is giggling and he's telling her loudly to be quiet. *TaDa!* He calls. The keys dangle in the door as it swings open with a slow whine to reveal his Dad in a small brown dressing gown and a large red frown. The girl struggles to pull a sober face and he starts laughing. His Dad stands to one side and points violently into the kitchen where they run inside and put chips in the oven. Dad's frown doesn't last long when he realises that he can eat chips without

Mum noticing. Together, they press their faces to the oven's warm
light and watch the chips become golden brown. He makes a
makeshift bed on the sofa for the girl, who runs into the bedroom
as soon as Dad has finished his share of the chips and gone to bed.
They curl up smiling. Our vision blurs.

After the soup, he makes her a cup of tea. He hesitates before
pulling out the packet of Hob Nobs and placing them diplomati-
cally on a coffee table between the two of them. In the morning, he
makes her another cup of tea, leaving it on his bedside table. She
waits in still silence while he gets dressed in a silk blue tie and grey
suit, then leaves for work. We stay in the house with her. We watch
her fold herself into the bath tub and half-fill it, the ends of her
long white-blonde hair swaying in the water like meadow grass in a
lazy summer breeze. We watch her pull on one of his carefully
ironed work shirts, the oily water from her skin seeping through
the expensive material and turning the pale blue into a darker hue.
She wanders around his house touching the furnishings, running
an oily finger along the wallpaper, leaving fingerprints on the 60-
inch wide screen television. Then she gets back into the bath and
turns on the water.

Time blurs and we see the patterns in her behaviour; baths,
wandering, the wearing of shirts. Time slows when he's home and
we watch him from the door of the kitchen, his lean back muscles
pushing through his shirt. He uses up his cupboard of beans and
Batchelors products and restocks with olive oils, herbs and fresh
chillies. She stands at the kitchen door too, watching his back
muscles ripple and twist. We cannot hear what he is saying, but he
talks quickly, he waves his hands around in the aroma of the food
he is cooking, or in the aroma of the story he is spilling. He turns
to see her reaction to his anecdote and is encouraged by the grey
face which does not respond, but which is looking at him.

We see him sleeping on the sofa, while she nestles in his bed.
She never sleeps, she only smiles secretly. No matter how many
extra blankets he piles on, she remains as cold as the day that he

found her. His water bills have tripled and he's started shopping at Waitrose. He takes the day he was owed to drive her to the seaside. He goes to work whistling. She never makes a sound. And she only ever smiles when he isn't in the room, or when his back is turned as he's cooking Thai curry and telling her about the people in the office.

One night, as he tosses and turns on the makeshift sofa bed and she twists herself into his bedsheets and blankets, our vision cuts to the other kitchen, the other time. The red haired girl is there, showing him maps and travel books. She looks wild and colourful in faded skinny jeans and an oversized royal blue jumper. He looks uneasy in a pale blue shirt and poorly done-up silk tie. He clutches his iPhone, the latest available, and leans away from the books and maps.

We see the red haired girl holding tickets up, waving them in his face and we see him putting on the silk tie again, tying it into a precise Oxford knot. He's already losing the smile.

We see the red haired girl, in different-coloured oversize jumpers, swirling around his kitchen, over-pouring his wine glass, lining up a travel itinerary that's printed on rough paper in scratchy ink.

We see a soundless argument in wild gestures. He throws maps across the kitchen table, she throws red wine over him and they both watch as the deep purple stain creeps across the pale blue fabric.

There's a short scene at an airport, where we see them hugging each other, holding onto each other tightly. The silk tie he is wearing is briefly caught in her red hair as she turns to leave.

We see him at the front door, the door to this house. His jaw is set firm. He dusts the new furniture and vacuums up the new carpet fluff. He plucks a few stray red hairs caught on his shirt and puts them in the bin. He goes shopping and buys tinned beans.

Tonight, our view is looking down onto the bed from the ceiling. The lights are off, but the glow of the street lamp creeps through the curtains. We see him wet and naked climb in beside her and pull at the sheets that she has wound around herself. She is not smiling. We see her eyes snap open and a human emotion seeps out from them. She begins to writhe as he tries to untangle her and then he's on top of her, towering over so that all we can see is his bare back, and his muscles twisting as he tries to get hold of her. She is hidden from view and we are powerless to help. Powerless, even, to bear witness. Fear is olfactory at a time like this. Through shafts of bone and skin, we can focus on his heart so that we do not have to see what is about to happen. Sinew and muscle and arteries are convulsing faster and faster and then they stop. And our vision pulls back and we can see her wrapped tight in the sheets, and he is on the floor by the night stand, blood moving quickly across his right hand which holds his head. He is the creature now, naked and alone and hurt, lying on the floor.

A warm orange morning light struggles through the kitchen window. From our view above the bed, we see him sit up. He's still on the floor, twisted in sheets streaked with oil and blood. The bed is empty. Time blurs again and our view swims through the house, following him, seeing him. He's dressed in a crumpled tee-shirt and jeans. We see him emptying the cupboards of fresh chillies and olive oils. But we see him replace them with nothing. We see him dust the softened furniture and vacuum the hardened carpets. We see him scrub a thin grey line in the bathtub and we see him, with a backpack, lock the door behind him and post the keys through the door. He's locked us in.

GREAT GRANDMOTHER'S STORIES

CROMWELL, Aotearoa New Zealand, 2219

Once upon a time, Great Grandmother told you stories.

Stories about a world – she said it was this world, only different – where the gulls would snatch children's food, but not their hands. Where humans were the top of the food chain and did whatever they wanted. Where they ate and drank from plastic wrap and plastic bottles and brushed their teeth with plastic brushes with paste that came in plastic tubes. Imagine! And the water was clean, she said, so clean you could drink it right from the source. You could even buy it, clean, in plastic bottles.

You're looking at one of these bottles now. The plastic is cleaner than you are. It's taken the weather better than you have. But you're getting older and everyone knows that people biodegrade eventually. Not like plastic.

You look at the gulls standing on the plastic oil can pile, about fifty paces to your right. There's three of them and their black, shining eyes don't betray which way they're looking. Their feet scrape and slap on the faded yellow plastic and they flap their wings, impatient for action. Maybe they know you're here. Maybe they're waiting.

It hasn't rained in days and the others sent you to find the lake, to bring back plastic bottles of water to purify and drink. It takes time to remove the micro-plastics and the chemical contaminants from the water. Camp water supplies are almost out and the others expected you back before the sun reached its peak. But there's been a delay. This small pack of gulls has been on your trail since dawn. You saw their dull brown outlines in the distance, specks above the mountains in the searing heat of high summer. The piles of plastic all around you are the perfect place to hide. Sticky fluid sits in the bottom of any plastic container that's still watertight and it all reeks so badly, you feel like it puts up a resistance, like you have to push your way through the air. But maybe that's hunger, dizziness, slowing you down.

Hunger speeds the gulls up. They're hunting. Great Grandmother told you a story about gulls eating scraps of human food, nibbling at things left behind because food was so plentiful back then that humans left a lot of things behind. They piled the left-behinds into big heaps that filled the land and the gulls would hover over the heaps and squawk loudly. Great Grandmother said the gulls didn't eat plastic back then, just the food scraps. The other kids didn't believe her. Gulls have always eaten the plastic and they need blood to dissolve plastic in their stomachs. Everybody knows that. But Great Grandmother insisted it was different in her day. She said humans made plastic – that humans loved plastic. That kids like you would play with moulded plastic inside nests made of blocks and concrete.

One of the gulls squawks a shriek of excitement and you worry for a moment that they've spotted you, but they're just fighting over a small, clear pottle with thick, red fluid swishing around the bottom of it. You swallow. Your throat is dry and you resist the urge to cough.

You take cover under a giant peach (that was a kind of fruit, once, and they weren't made of plastic, Great Grandmother said). Tall pillars with remnants of other giant fruits huddle around it, but the giant peach is the only whole landmark discernible for miles. The others told you there was water not far from here – half a day wading through the plastic heaps at the most. But since the gulls showed up you've been reluctant to move from the peach. One gull can cause a nasty injury, one that could get infected. Three gulls could overwhelm someone of your stature. Picking and scraping at your eyes and mouth, they'd dig with their thin-webbed and tiny-clawed feet until they drew blood and then the frenzy would begin.

You had a sister once. When you were younger she liked to dig through the heaps to find scraps of food and she'd concentrate so hard the whole world around her would disappear. She didn't hear when the gulls came and the other kids screamed and ran for cover under the rocks.

Great Grandmother was still alive then too. She cried. A waste of good water, crying like that, the others said. But she cried anyway. That's when she told you about the gulls in her time, the ones that would steal scraps of food, but food wasn't so scarce so humans didn't mind. Sometimes, they'd throw food to the gulls, just to watch them fight each other. The way they'd hover, then dive. Hover, then dive. She told you so many stories about her time – the others told you they were fantasies. Humans couldn't have made a world like this, they told you, look at our soft bodies, our small eyes and thin limbs, humans could not have made the plastic, could not have killed trees and filled lakes of clean water with dirt and poison and plastic. Humans are simple and innocent crea-tures, they told you. But you wondered about Great Grandmoth-er's stories. Stories about humans with machines that took them great distances in short times, about huge places with lines and lines of food neatly wrapped in little plastic packages to take when-ever you wanted them. With lights that shone at night and machines that moved through the air faster than the gulls. You

loved her stories, back then. They took you to a place that felt safe
and warm and full.

You shift from lying on your stomach to kneeling. The gulls
have their backs to you and they've moved slightly further away. It
could be a trick – gulls are clever hunters – but they seem absorbed
by the pottle with the red stuff in it. They're fighting among themselves and making a lot of noise. You stand up and put a hand on
the peach. The ground below you moves and slides beneath your
feet. It's made of flattened plastic. The top parts are pastel-
coloured, but you can see other plastics below in their brighter, un-
sun-bleached glory. The heap you're standing on slopes down-
wards and in the distance, there appears to be a drop-off. This
could be the water, you think. It'll be hidden underneath a layer of
floating plastic – this long, flat layer is a tell-tale sign of water.

The sun is low and hot. You draw long, shallow, shaky breaths
and feel dizzy. Long, shallow, shaky breaths. Long, shallow, shaky
breaths. If you fall asleep beneath the peach, the gulls might find
you. You're not used to sleeping by yourself and the idea makes
you feel soft-fleshed, like a rat caught on its back, with its bloated,
pink belly in the air for all to pick at. You remember your sister and
she reminds you to concentrate.

You're not sure when you decided to do this, but now you're
running, no, sliding, across the pile of plastics. You're on your feet
most of the time, but occasionally, you bruise your arms and sides
rolling and sliding sideways down the heap. A shrill cry breaks out
behind you. The faded-pastel-coloured plastics paint a colourful
blur all around you as you run, stumble and tumble down. Your
foot hits something solid, something metal, and you feel blood
rushing. You hope the blood is not leaking out, not leaving a bright
red trail behind you. The gulls would smell that, the gulls would
find you then.

Through the blur, you can see the plastic has started to move
with you. Pottles and plastic cans, sticky tumbleweed balls of thin,
clear plastic and a bright blue piece in the shape of an animal with

a flat tail and a long, rounded nose, chase you down the slope. You and the plastic are gathering more speed now. Sometimes you're up, running with your legs, other times you're down again, sliding on your side or your back. You see a brown shadow swoop for your head and miss. They are here. They're silent because they're serious. They've eaten their fill of plastic and now they need your blood to help them digest. Everything is moving at speed, so you only see pastel-multi-colours and flashes of dark brown, but you can imagine their distended stomachs and hooked beaks.

At once, everything is shockingly cold and you gasp for air, but none of it comes. You feel your insides clench and your immediate thought is that the gulls have pierced your flesh and this is what dying feels like. You float to the surface and spit out water, managing to swallow enough air to submerge yourself again, moving in the water instinctively, though you have never seen this much water before. This is it, this is the lake, you're here.

The water stings your open eyes, but you see a large piece of soft plastic floating nearby. The gulls penetrate the water, diving sharply near you. One of them bites your leg and again, you feel the rush of blood and this time you see red, smoke-like trails clouding the water around the fresh wound. The soft plastic is thick, thick enough to soften the blow of the gulls, but soft enough to move and wrap around you so that the gulls get caught in it as they try to dive for you. They start to take it in turns to dive for your head, pushing your face underwater so that you have to breathe fast, taking in air whenever you can. You can't breathe under the water and this sparks a novel thought: you might die under the water. And you'll be the first person you know who dies from too much water.

You bunch up more of the sheeting around your body, like a blanket. You notice that you're holding the plastic creature, the blue one with a flat tail and a long, rounded nose. You must have snatched it up as you tumbled through the heaps, and you're not sure why, but it's comforting to hold.

It reminds you of another of Great Grandmother's stories. The one about the swimming pool. A neat rectangle of blue water, with plastic playthings floating in it, back when humans floated in water for fun. Great Grandmother would wrap plastic around her arms and use them to help her swim in the water. The water couldn't be drunk – it was filled with chemicals so you couldn't drink it. It was just for fun.

You grab onto a large bottle floating next to you, to help you float. The gulls are still diving and for now, you're still floating. You don't know how to swim, you don't know how to keep floating. So you hug the blue plastic animal and the plastic bottle, and you close your eyes and hold your breath each time a gull pushes your head into the water.

It's this water, this unbreathable water that will kill you and the gulls know it, they knew it before you did. You hold tighter onto the bottle as a gull dives for your head again and small pieces of floating plastic brush your cheeks. The soft plastic is still protecting you, so you'll stay like this until the gulls stop or you stop breathing.

Live by the plastic, die by the plastic – Great Grandmother said that once and you make a mental note to ask her what it means when you join her in the place after this one.

THE PROGRAMME

Do you remember how The Programme came to be? I do. I've gone over and over the video clips and compiled files on every episode. I've done my research. I've gone deeper than any mega-fan.

When the concept for The DBL Programme was first advertised, the people complained. The headlines spelt out that we'd reached a new low. Who would watch that? Who would condone it? Even criminals deserve basic human rights, they said.

#BanDBL was trending. Hackers managed to deface digital advertising with calls for moderation. Even a few politicians stood against it, but, ultimately, they said the people would decide. The DBL Programme wasn't against the law. Public executions had been reintroduced over a decade ago, ushered in by a small but vocal group of extreme-thinking, moderate-sounding opinion piece writers and new wave religious leaders who had their cash-filled hands in the right pockets. But when The Programme first started, the idea of a televised DBL execution was hard for the people to stomach.

And then came the Casus incident. Do you remember him? Few do these days, though occasionally his name will pop up in pub quizzes held in dimly lit, nicotine-stained bars. But back then, Casus crashed into our news feeds with uncanny timing. His image coming up every second thumb-flick, haunting our LCD screens.

Appearing on The Programme catapults people into a new kind of celebrity status. We remember their story, their face, their crime. For a week or two, at least. That's a long half-life in the online world. I didn't get involved in any of it, not back then, anyway. I was a bystander, casually observing and keeping a vague tally of the details like one might with their second favourite football team. But I've done my research since. I know every episode now. I've gone deeper than any mega-fan.

Casus was the perfect poster boy for The Programme. An immigrant with a foreign accent – or so they told us in the pilot episode. His eyes were a deep brown and in all the photos, he was squinting like a light was shining in his face. *What evil eyes*, the people said. *The eyes of a terrorist*, they said, as though a human's soul could be judged purely on prison photos.

His trial only took a few days, the jury was unanimous in his guilt and the sentence was handed down.

'Death by Like.'

His was the first televised Death by Like execution. After the episode aired, the fundamentalists cried out in joy. Like for like. An eye for an eye. Or in the Casus case – death by suitcase.

He had no family, or at least none the media could find. Colleagues at the fast-food restaurant where Casus had worked some time ago could not remember much about him. He was quiet, did not go out drinking like them, did not dress like them, talk like them. He'd left the fast-food restaurant to become a free-lance web developer, picking up bits of work on internet job boards. Neighbours said he didn't leave the house, that the only visitors were delivery people and posties.

He was the perfect poster boy. Too perfect, too convenient, some might have said, but most didn't.

They said he built a bomb out of nails and household chemicals. He hid it in a suitcase and carried it to a shopping centre, then left it in the atrium just after lunchtime. The bomb killed a woman and her two children. They were all blonde, beautiful creatures. The bomb killed their dog too. A golden retriever. Golden retrievers never have suspect-looking eyes in pictures.

The father was a war veteran. He cried on TV.

They say 3.4 million tuned in to watch the Casus episode. They made a replica shopping centre atrium with holograms of people walking by and potted trees twitching in an airconditioned breeze. The show included interviews with survivors and friends and family of the deceased beautiful blondes, with a self-styled 'expert psychologist' trying to fill in Casus's mindset and motives. The whole time, Dan Casus sat there by the suitcase, shaking. He didn't, or couldn't, move. Then, forty-six minutes into the programme, they set the bomb off. I think I've watched that moment a hundred times. The camera shake, the grey dust clouds that settled to reveal a dark streak across the atrium floor. The detritus of the birth of a new era in capital punishment and enter-tainment.

The #BanDBL movement slowed to a crawl. There was a handful of protests in the streets where photojournalists zoomed their cameras in to make the crowds look crowded. A few outspoken journalists asked questions, to which nobody wanted to hear the answers. The producers were ready with their arguments: that it was no more graphic than *CSI* or *Game of Thrones*, that even *Eastenders* deals with more tragedy and human woe in each episode. Politicians colluded; 'this is the best thing for the security of our country'. Bloggers quoted each other as 'research' and said statistics showed it would help with our spiralling 'terrorist prob-lem'. A catchphrase was coined and people wrote it on cardboard signs, hash-tagged it and chanted it in the streets: *This Is What Justice Looks Like*. It popped up in memes. Big brands sided with The Programme in boosted social media posts.

Funding must have come from somewhere. The Programme's

supporters must have had money. Did anyone think about that? Did you? At the time, I didn't. But I've done my research now. I've gone deeper than any mega-fan. I've thought a lot about how an idea for a TV series takes ages to pitch and write and longer to make. Without the high-tech holograms and the carefully built sets (and bombs), we'd have looked like one of those other countries – the over-zealous ones who are always executing people and chucking it on YouTube, or so it seems. No. We didn't want to do it like that. We wanted to savour the kill with carefully picked motion graphics and a theme tune that John Williams would have been proud of. And a male narrator's voice that had the authority of David Attenborough and the smoothness of Morgan Freeman. This doesn't come cheap. The financial backing was always there. I've come to the conclusion that The Programme was always going to happen. Dan Casus was just our first victim.

The hyperbole around the Casus episode created the perfect storm for the second. Millions tuned in. Millions. They bludgeoned to death a pasty, skinny twenty-three-year-old who'd supposedly murdered his three-year-old step-daughter. Pictures of her in pink welly boots and a yellow rain jacket flashed up on the screen before big, masked men walked into a mock-up living room with bats. It doesn't take as long as you'd think to bludgeon someone to death.

There were women, too. Do you remember them? Child killers, vengeful wives and a wayward nurse who'd deliberately overdosed her elderly patients. I think they used something different to overdose the nurse – froth dribbled down her chin and onto the collar of her dress and she writhed like she had an itch somewhere awkward. I can't imagine a real overdose being like that, but TV needs to be bolder and brighter than real life, doesn't it?

By the end of the first season, The Programme was part of everyday life. It was talked about in workplace tea rooms and the tabloids pored over the details when there weren't any other scandals to write about. They say crime rates are down, but it could be because more people are watching TV these days. They're live streaming The Programme or watching spin-off interviews. Posting their half-stewed thoughts on Facebook or arguing on Twitter about the top three most ugly deaths and which dead Programme crim they'd like to date, if they could. A well-subscribed YouTube gamer started a TikTok dance-off to the theme tune and within a week, politicians were joining in, hoping to pick up election points.

I didn't pay attention to the dance-offs, spin-offs and memes. I didn't really watch The Programme unless there was nothing good on Netflix. That was until they got Jake. Though they didn't call him that. They found his birth name, it was more foreign-sounding. Like Casus, he had the right 'look' for a TV-anointed terrorist. One of his foster families had been devoutly religious and Jake had half-heartedly kept up the habit, but The Programme said he was a fanatic. They interviewed some of his other foster families and the Home, who all remembered an angry, troubled boy. I remember a man who'd overcome his past, was actively grappling with his future and determined to create a better life for himself. For us both.

I appealed to my friends, my family to help. But the vision The Programme had created was too strong. Whether there was real evidence to prove his guilt didn't matter; whoever writes the memes writes history. And the pundits were hungry. Jake's clipped way of talking suddenly became evidence of an angry, dark side that had been brewing.

There was a short section on me. I declined to be interviewed – Jake's lawyer said it was a bad idea. My dad fronted and said I'd fallen for bad boys before. Even if he'd said Jake was different, they'd have cut it. In the papers, I was described as a 'sweet, bubbly girl' and an image of sixteen-year-old me wearing a boob-tube with my hair bleached-blonde and straightened to paper-like consistency kept doing the rounds in the magazines and online.

It didn't help that Jake and I had been arguing. I'd already told Mum and a few friends we were on the verge of a break-up. I'd left a few strident-independent-female type memes on various social media platforms. Family and friends saw it as my cry for help, that I'd been struggling to leave a bad relationship and a dangerous man. Truth is, I wanted to move to Ibiza for a year. He wanted kids. He always was the more mature one, the one striving for a safe, secure life. They killed him with sarin because they couldn't get Novichok. I didn't watch, but I heard it was a slow death. I've watched every episode since.

That was seven years ago. Nobody remembers Jake now either. Even Mum and Dad have lost Jake in a blur of ex-boyfriends. I went to Ibiza. I ruined myself on drugs, regularly. I read every conspiracy theory about The Programme. I re-watched all the previous episodes apart from Jake's, poring over every detail, pausing explosions and watching poisonings in slow-motion.

I started an online relationship with an American conspiracy writer who lived in Spain. His name is Robert Smith. He claimed to be a full-time theorist, but I knew he worked part-time at a souvenir shop. I lived with him in Spain for four months and we came up with my plan while smoking weed one night. It was simple, clean, boring. Patience was the key to it. He came up with a lot of the key steps, I added the flourishes. Only one of us was serious that night, I think.

I married him for his simple, common name. He married me for an easy visa. It suited both of us and when we left Spain, we parted ways with the casual attitude of two people walking in different directions down the same supermarket aisle.

He went on to become a newspaper journalist in the city, just like he said he would, though he was covering the Business Desk and not Crime like he'd wanted to. I moved back in with my parents and took a Masters in Communications. I didn't unpack my boxes and I kept my make-up on the floor by the mirror. My parents were thrilled I was coming around, pulling myself together. The bubbly blonde was back. I took an internship, then a job at the television station. I was promoted to Social Media Lead and I kept everyone entertained with posts just scandalous enough to gain followers for the company, but not worry our law team. The people who worked on The Programme kept to themselves, they preferred to run their own social pages. So I started collating reports for them, pointing out memes and new blog posts about changes in algorithms. Flirting with the producer and spontaneously joining their table at the staff cafeteria like I was always one of the team. I flaunted my in-depth knowledge of The Programme. It took two-and-a-half years of playing the bubbly, blonde social media gal to get here: The Programme's office party, take two.

The party will be starting soon, they're even playing the same Spotify playlist as the one we had that night. I know because I created it, I remember every song. The balloons are the wrong shade of blue, but I suppose I'm the only one who'll notice these details.

Everything else is the same. The set designer couldn't make it to the actual office party, so I'm guessing he's been the one to carefully reconstruct the office – the navy swivel chairs, cream and grey desks with dual screens balanced on gleaming silver stands everywhere. The low, white ceiling. The lack of windows. The large gas heaters I brought in after cutting the power to the air con. The room is smaller than the actual office and I'm able to walk around if I want to. They usually do this for the slower, quieter deaths in the hope that the Accused will panic and try to escape – it's better viewing that way.

A voice comes crisp and clear through the set: *Rose Ophelia Smith, you have been sentenced to Death by Like. This Is What Justice Looks Like.* I know I won't hear anything else – the interviews or dramatizations, just my carefully designed playlist.

It's getting hot, so I pull off my top and sit in my sports bra and skinny black jeans. We're in the entertainment industry, after all.

I sink back into the chair and slowly plait my hair over my shoulder. It's just like I've always dreamed. The music begins to swell and holograms start to swirl around the room. They've given me a glass of sparkling water, tinted slightly to look like champagne – I nod 'cheers' in the direction of where I think one of the cameras will be.

I didn't spend long with Robert, but I know him well enough. He'll have spilt my story to the media. About Jake, about my drug-addled time in Ibiza and Spain, about my long-held secret vendetta against The Programme. He'll have carefully left out the part where this was mostly his idea and the part where he married me for a visa. But I think he'll write our story well: he'll show the world what The Programme really is and who is really behind it – and why. After all, this is Robert's express ticket to the career in hard crime journalism that he's long wanted.

I look around at the holograms surrounding me. They haven't obscured anyone's identity, everyone looks as they should. The holographic producer walks up to me with a ghostly smile and stares with what should have been a piercing look, but the holo-gram flickers at just the wrong time. A flaw in their programming. I smile and nod cheers to him, too, then breathe in deeply.

You can't smell or taste carbon monoxide, that's what is so good about it. And it's far easier to get hold of than Novichok.

I make myself comfortable on the chair, careful to position myself at just the right angle so that when I fall down dead, the cameras will see my tattoos. I have two: 'Is This Really What Justice Looks Like?' and Jake's full name. In case people don't join the dots and Robert doesn't perform the way I expect him to. I've made a backup plan. I've written a search-engine-optimised blog post explaining all. I've scheduled it to be published around about now, set up some digital advertising for it and I've pre-made a bunch of memes and follow-up posts for social media. You could say I've made good use of my education.

I'm feeling dizzy and a headache is starting to seep from my temples into my neck. I can smell burnt toast, but I don't remember there being a toaster in the room.

I had wanted the notoriety, I used to fantasise about the fame.

About what people like Robert would write about me after I died.

The ridiculousness of how my death will be portrayed, compared to Casus, or Jake. I'd even thought about screaming and flailing around and putting on a bit of a show. But now I'm here, I don't care anymore. I've done my research. I've gone deeper than any mega-fan. I've done my time. And now, I'm looking forward to the sick fluoresce of LCD screens finally going dark and a deep, deep sleep.

DATING LIFE

DEATH FELL ON DEAF EARS, like she so often does.

'For Christ's sake, can you just stop it?' She hissed. Her patience wearing thin and frayed like the carpet in the hall. Soiled, abused, much-trodden-on.

She rattled the battered toaster and mopped up the burnt crumbs with a dishcloth that smelled of old damp. Death twisted her thin lips, then let out a sigh. She turned to face the kitchen, letting the edge of the bench press into the small of her back.

Morning sunshine played on the grubby white kitchen tiles and her two children sat at opposite ends of a centuries-old wooden table eating breakfast. Death ran the silver chain of her pocket watch through her fingers and snapped open the clasp. She wouldn't have time for breakfast today.

Moving with purpose down the hall, she closed the mess of each room behind heavy wooden doors. She grabbed the washing basket from the bathroom and used a school jumper to mop up a puddle on the floor, then she threw the washing into the utility room and closed the door on that too. In her bedroom, she hastily straightened the navy bedsheets and kicked a pile of self-help books and dream journals under the bed. She brushed the ancient Persian rug with her feet, kicking out a few wrinkles and bringing a semblance of colour back to the worn pile. She spritzed her favourite perfume all around the room.

In the kitchen, Truth flicked another cornflake at his baby sister, Fallacy. This time, the cornflake hit her in the eye and though it didn't hurt a bit, she howled with all the ferocity of a spring storm.

'Oh, for the love of God!' Death said, thundering down the hall, lifting Fallacy from her high chair and sweeping back her strawberry blonde curls.

Truth ruffled his own mess of jet black curls and snorted. He wore his favourite faded black tee-shirt with the word 'NO' emblazoned on the front and baggy jeans that desperately clung to his protruding hips and hung limply over his arse.

Death shot a fierce look at her son, feeling both perplexed and amazed at the lanky young man he was quickly becoming. 'What?' he said, petulantly, 'She always over-reacts, Mum!'

'And that gives you the right to wind her up, does it? Does it?'

Death exhaled, then smiled. She looped Truth closer to her with her free arm and kissed him on the forehead. He didn't embrace her, like he would have, once, but for a moment he leaned into the kiss and breathed in Death's scent. Fallacy stopped howling and rested her heavy head on Death's collarbone.

'Sorry, Mum. Sorry, Folly,' he mumbled, and affectionately stroked Fallacy's arm.

Fallacy giggled. Despite their difference in years, Truth and Fallacy were very fond of each other.

'Right, I'm fucking off. Smell you losers later.'

'Truth! Watch your goddamn mouth for Christ's sake!'

Truth snorted again; 'Hey, I'm going to Dad's tonight for tea, yeah?'

'Yep. Let me know when you're heading back home, okay?'

Truth didn't answer. He raised his hand in half-surrender, half-goodbye and slung his school bag over his shoulder. He pulled open the front door with more strength than he'd expected and it bashed against the hallway wall, accentuating the dent that was already there.

'Fuckssake,' hissed Death.

'Sorry, Mum,' Truth called, sauntering, slightly bow-legged, down the garden path. He'd take the scenic route, be late for school again, and Death would have to field a call from the head-mistress later.

Fallacy resumed howling.

Death's gaze rested on a yellow rose, newly blooming, in her wild front garden. Clipping it with an old scythe she kept in an umbrella stand by the front door, Death placed it, thorns and all, in an old vase on her bedside table.

Then, gathering a squirming Fallacy into her arms, Death headed out into the world.

Death carefully lifted the hem of her navy velvet cloak away from the jaws of the escalator. The sick fluorescent lights above her flickered and as she watched the filthy, graffiti-covered wall tiles slide sluggishly by her, she thought about how the descent into this shopping centre was not unlike the descent into hell.

The atmosphere was unpleasant, sure, but she loved the play centre that was tucked away in a bottom corner. The play centre's outdoor space was marked out by commercial bins that reeked of vomit and most of the dolls there had had their faces drawn back on by two-year-old artists. But Death thought the world of Mrs Dunbarr, the seventy-something Scottish woman who ran the centre.

Mrs Dunbarr probably wasn't allowed to run a play centre anymore. But in all the playschools in this world and the next, she was the kindest and most accepting woman Death had ever met. And Death would not trust her precious Fallacy to anyone else.

Fallacy squealed in delight as Death handed her over to Mrs Dunbarr.

'Ach, full of energy this wee one. You have a good day at work now, Miss Lucy.'

'Thanks, Mrs Dunbarr. Mum's picking her up tonight.'

'Oh, yes? You're not off out the night, are you? Meeting him again?'

Death's stare said it all.

'Ach. Take it from an auld woman, Miss Lucy, you're better off without that bampot.'

Death smiled and gave Fallacy a childish wave, then headed back into the shopping centre atrium.

Between a shoe repair shop and a tacky card shop was the bakery. A large man sat outside with a four-pack of steak bakes. Flakes of pastry cascaded between his fingers and onto his tracksuit bottoms. A pigeon eyed him worriedly from the sticky tiled floor. A blue and orange advertisement for the bakery's latest meal deal glared above the man's head: a vegan sausage roll, a piece of fruit and a cup of tea for £4.

He saw her glance at him and pulled a face. She hurried past and ordered the meal deal at the counter, where the young woman asked if she'd like milk and sugar in her tea.

'No. Black tea please,' she handed over her favourite black reusable cup, given to her by Fallacy's dad. It had taken a few months to dig beneath the memories of betrayal back to the cup's origins – a small, unexpected gift and a damn good cup that didn't make tea taste like plastic.

Clutching the cup, a paper bag and an orange, Death headed back towards the atrium.

'Bit old to be dressing like a bloody Goth, aren't ya, lovvie?' the man hollered, and waited for her reply.

'Oi! I'm talking to you, Goth whore.'

Death jostled her breakfast into her floral cloth saddlebag as the escalator elevated her into the cool daylight. With her now free left hand, she snapped her fingers and didn't bother to look back as screams of surprise erupted behind her.

Others leaned over the escalator handrails to watch the young woman from the bakery attempt CPR on the large man. Death sighed. It was going to be a long day.

Death examined the uppers of her black Piñatex boots. The admin assistant, Acedia, was wearing strong, cheap deodorant and it was making her feel light-headed. The ceiling fan throbbed above them as he listlessly clicked his mouse and basked in the glow of his LCD computer screen.

'Huh, I don't think it's here.'

'Acedia, it IS there. Under Deaths, click this century and the files should be in date order.'

Death grabbed the corner of his screen and jabbed her finger at the offending file.

'There.'

'Gotcha. There's still only 48,742 on this list, though. Wait, it says 48,742 *plus one*... did you already take someone this morning?'

'There has to be more,' said Death, tapping her tablet and hoping more names would magically appear.

Acedia looked dreamily at his screen again and made a long, quiet, high-pitched humming sound. Death slammed her tablet down onto the desk and stood up quickly, sending the flimsy plastic chair she'd been sitting on tumbling backwards.

Death looked at the smile spreading across Acedia's acne-marked face. She jumped as two hot hands came down heavy on her shoulders and she realised Acedia was not smiling at her.

'Life! You scared me.'

She felt her stomach fold itself up neatly and hide behind her ribcage. Her cheeks grew warm and Death hoped her pale foundation would hide the colouration.

'Sweetheart! Looks like you have a short day at work today.'

'Somebody here must know where the rest of my list is. There cannot be only 48,742 deaths on Earth today. I want to speak to the Powers That Be.'

The ceiling fan thudded louder and rows of admin assistants looked up from the glow of their LCD screens. As a principal player, Death was physically larger than the assistants. In her heeled boots, she towered over Acedia's desk and she could easily be seen from the other side of the corridor-like office.

Life, her equal and opposite, threw back his head and laughed. The assistants relaxed and several began clicking and staring deep into their computers again.

'Sweetheart, this really doesn't need to be escalated. Just stick to the list and take it easy, yeah?'

Acedia nodded his head vigorously; 'Tomorrow's list is back up to around 150,000. I don't think you're going to have a big backlog if that's what you're worried about.'

Death righted the chair and hissed at Acedia.

'That's exactly the opposite of what I'm worried about. This is the third short list this month. And Life's list keeps getting longer. Where are the checks and balances? What will happen when every inch of Earth is crawling with human life? It's not sustainable.' Life laughed again.

'Oh, you greenies, you make me laugh. Leave Acedia be. The list is the list. The Powers That Be know what they're doing.

You just do your job, yeah, sweetheart? And I'll see you tonight,' Life winked at her, then gave the room a big, over-dramatic wave. A few of the assistants smiled and waved back.

Death readjusted her cloak and shouldered her saddlebag.

'Fine,' she said, quietly.

'Is there anything further I can help you with today?' asked Acedia, quickly followed by 'have a nice day, Ma'm' as Death pressed the toes of her boots into the carpet tiles, spun around and strode towards the office doors with a swish of her navy cloak.

. . .

'Right this way, Miss,' the waiter gestured to an orange-varnished table with an ill-fitting white table cloth over it.

Death followed him to the table and looked down on the arrangement, her eyes lingering on a greasy thumbprint on one of the knives.

'Do you have any other tables? Something a little larger... and maybe not so close to the toilets?' she added, drawing herself up to let past a man who was still adjusting his fly.

'I'll let you know if something becomes available,' the waiter said, his open palm still gesturing to the wooden chairs. So she sat down and polished the knife on the edge of the table cloth, knowing the waiter would forget all about it.

Life was always running late. He stumbled in, dressed as gaudily as ever: a short-sleeved shirt emblazoned with palm trees and big, orange-beaked toucans, tan chinos and blue suede shoes. A pair of sunglasses held back a mess of gold and silver hair. The beginnings of a moustache threatened his upper lip.

Death's stomach tumbled and a cold shiver crept across her skin. She pulled back an elated smile into a polite one.

'Lucy, sweetheart!' Life said, grabbing her shoulders and kissing her on both cheeks. 'It's great to see you, sweetheart. Like, really good.'

Death couldn't decide if he sounded surprised or conceited.

'I think it's good to keep the connection, for Fallacy's sake,' said Death, a little more curtly than she'd intended.

'And how is she?'

'Oh, she's trouble. It's just her age. She's staying with Mum tonight.'

'Is... is Truth there too?'

'No, he's at his dad's. But they're honestly great together, most of the time.'

'Hmm.'

'Truth's actually a great help around the house. He's great with Fallacy. He's growing up fast. And, you know, now she's getting a little older, there's nothing stopping you from taking care of Fallacy, from time to time. If a teenager can do it, well...'

Life took hold of Death's wrists and turned her hands so that they rested palm-up in his hot grip. Death felt as though she was having her palms read, her fortune spelt out to her. She suddenly felt warm, excited in Life's firm hold.

'It's your night off, sweetheart! You don't want to talk about your kids on your night off. What else has been happening?'

'Just work... and I don't suppose you want to talk about that, do you?'

Death looked directly into his pupils and Life let go of her hands.

'Aha. Well, after this morning's little display, I did notice you'd been busy. Gary, outside of the bakery, I didn't know he was on your list?'

'Everyone is on my list.'

'Aha, ha. Yes, but perhaps you were a tad early there?'

'Does it matter? Amy in the bakery will go on to become a paramedic, triggered by that experience. She'll transform her own life, save others. You're all about that right?'

The waiter interrupted them with the starters. Death slowly pulled her dough balls apart and watched the olive oil rise and creep into the bread's soft insides. Life tore into his chicken wings and rubbed BBQ sauce onto the tablecloth with his fingers.

'Do you ever think about that, Gabe?'

'What?'

A piece of chicken spat from between Life's teeth onto his plate. Death felt a wave of repulsion and gladness. She couldn't take her eyes off him, but she saw Life in all his glory and folly again.

She sat up straighter in her chair and fortified her voice.

'All of this life. It's everywhere, Gabe. So much of it. There's an awful lot of people out there. Don't you think Earth is getting a bit...'

A woman squeezed past their table, holding in her rolls of stomach to prevent it from tugging at their tablecloth. Death and Life smiled politely at her.

'Squeezed?' Life laughed.

'Exactly. I'm not asking you to spill trade secrets or anything... but is there a plan... a plan for all of this life? It just seems so wasteful, that's all.'

Life laughed again. His laugh was heavenly, like distant holy bells on a Sunday morning. Death remembered how much she'd hated that laugh, especially after sex.

'You're not being, uh, work-shy there are you Lucy?'

She raised her hand and extended her fingers, ready to give him a two-fingered fuck-off gesture, but Life saw it as a threat to snap her fingers.

'Whoa, I'm joking. You've already done more than your quota today. Listen, leave it to me, yeah? When have I ever let you down?'

His neat white teeth were sticky with BBQ sauce. She spent the rest of the meal simmering in a polite rage.

Crisp packets leaned precariously towards her and the magazine rack threatened to send an avalanche of glossy tits cascading across the narrow floor space. Somewhere, a radio carried the voice of the country's current leader. He intoned the importance of addressing climate change, speaking in a mixture of lacklustre English and Ancient Greek in an accent that grated on her.

Death found her favourite Merlot on a dusty shelf near the back.

'I think it's out of date, love,' said the shopkeeper, pointing to the bottle's excellent vintage, unavailable anywhere else in this world or the next.

Death handed over a dirty twenty pound note. She could see

the shopkeeper's life sprawling around her greasy hair in a muddy yellow aura. There was a sickness there, unhappiness. She could see the woman's passion for the sound of the viola, an instrument she'd never get to touch. And she could see her family; the lazy husband obsessed with betting on his horses and the two sons whom she loved so much, but her love was unrequited. Death could not see an end to the woman's miserable timeline. She resisted the urge to take her under her navy cloak and carry her to the underworld.

'I like it this way. Keep the change, spend it on your boys,' Death smiled at the shopkeeper.

She pulled her cloak tighter around her shoulders to stop it from dragging along the grimy flagstones and patched concrete. Taxis and Ubers huffed along the narrow roads, leaving behind the stench of exhaust fumes that Death had come to associate as the overriding flavour of the 21st Century. A man with a beige corduroy coat slept on a pile of plastic bags in a scorched and boarded-up doorway. Death watched another man, dressed in a sharp grey suit, hurry towards the man in the doorway. Death could see they'd been born on the same day, in this same city. Both were handsome, in an Ancient Greek sort of way. She let their life timelines spiral out before her in trails of deep purple and black smoke. She watched how their timelines twisted and changed, how Fortune and Fate had toyed with their lives. Then she looked at their souls and saw how different they were. One filled with contentedness and purpose, causing a ball of smoke that pulsed different deep, rich colours. The other man's soul churned bright but off-colour hues, he was filled with fear and sadness.

Death snapped her fingers and the man appeared before her, his edges softened by the smoke-like form he had become. She dusted away the ugly colours from his soul.

'It's okay,' she whispered, 'I'll take you home.'

He fell into her arms and ran the pads of his fingers up and down the soft velvet of her cloak like a distracted child. Behind him, the man in the beige coat woke with a start and crawled over to the body of the man in the grey suit.

At home, Death poured herself generous glasses of wine. She made sure she drank enough to give herself a mild headache. She walked around the house from room to room, drinking in the silence, taking in the mess of her life. Her heart strained against the disorder.

Loneliness clung to her navy velvet cloak.

Finally, she peered into her bedroom from the door and inspected her hasty efforts. The room smelled like her favourite perfume and the yellow rose had unfurled its petals in an open embrace of the room. Death sighed at her own wishful, thoughtless thinking. She didn't want Life, not again, not anymore.

TIGER FOOD

SHE GRABS the crumpled letter from the waste paper basket when she thinks that no one is watching. She grabs her coat, her red hat and her reading folder (or she'll get detention again). Before she swings her bag, one-shouldered onto her back (it's pink, with 101 Dalmatians on it... although she's not really counted), she hides the letter in the secret side pocket that's reserved for special things. As she walks, a spoon drums against her lunch box. She's walking fast on short legs into the corridor and into the yard. The spoon beats the beat with each stone step stepped upon and the girls skip ropes while the boys play ball.

Crack, crack, crack.

The ropes. *Boom, boom,* the bass of the ball. And the s*lap-slap-slap* of loose rubber sole shoes on concrete slabs. And really, there's a thousand heartbeats but they're all rolled into one.

But the spoon beats faster, playing out of time. She feels everyone's eyes on her, but all she sees are buckled shoes and gum-freckled concrete and the odd lonely little stone in the distance. It's just outside of the school gates that she runs into Frank. She would have kept on running but there's something about giant, orange tiger paws that stand out among the Clarks lace-ups and the Buckle-My-Shoes.

'H-hello.'

'Grrroood afternoon, and who might you be?'

'Baranina... wh-wh-what's your name?'

'Frrrank.'

Baranina is quick to notice Frank's Blue Peter badge. She's not afraid, you can never be afraid of anyone who has a Blue Peter badge. When she's older, she'll work on Blue Peter and have a gold Blue Peter badge.

'What's the matter, Barrranina?' Frank looks directly into her red, wet face.

'I-I-I'mmm in trouble a-a-a-gain. M-m-mrs Huller told me off-f-f f-for daydreaming.'

There's salty water everywhere and her nose runs freely into her mouth which pipes it back up to her eyes. Now that he's noticed, it suddenly seems perfectly acceptable for her to make a mess of herself. So she does. If she blinks, the water makes little drop-shaped badges on her pinafore. These are not Blue Peter badges; these are nothing to be proud of.

'Here, mop yourrr face clean.' (Frank has an old-fashioned cotton hankie.)

'Th-th-tha-'

'You'rrre Welcome.'

A green bubble begins to blossom from her nose before Baranina can capture it with the handkerchief. It grows and grows and grows until it's so big, it falls from her face and drops gently towards the ground. A gust of wind catches it, and it floats up and up and up towards the tops of lampposts and it climbs the sky until it's higher than the chimneys and the broken roof tiles. It floats away from the school, hovering above the estate for a moment before turning East, and heading off towards Africa, or maybe China to see the panda bears.

'That letter, little Barrranina...'

'Oh, how-how do you know?'

'I saw that nasty owl deliverrr it. I just thought I'd warrrn you, you shouldn't accept letters off strangerrrs, whether they're fluffy snowy owls orr not.'

'I-i-it says that I'm special, that I could go to a magical school for people just like m-me... but Mrs Huller says I've made it all up, that I'm daydreaming again.'

'Indeed! She sounds like a rude woman.'

'Sh-she is! She is!'

'Howeverrr, Is it really wise to go off to some strrrange school that a ruddy owl invited you to? Would it not be wiserr to finish your SATs exams first, at least?'

'I-I-I suppose.'

She starts to walk home, and Frank pads along beside her in big, long strides. No one else seems to notice Frank, apart from the sparrows who shriek and hide in the bushes. She thinks it would be polite to talk, he does seem like a really clever tiger, aaand he doesn't think she made the owl and the letter up.

'Wh-wh-where do you live?' She's not seen Frank before.

He probably lives in a different estate.

'Rrrussia'

'Oh', Baranina has not heard of that estate, they're usually named after women writers around here, 'Do you have a long way to walk, then?'

'It's quite farrr', He smiles, a simple, line-drawn smile. 'I shall have to stop to eat something on the way.'

'Fr-frank...'

'Yes?'

'Would you like to come for tea?'

'Sounds delightful, little Barrranina!'

Baranina loves to have friends over for tea. Mum and Dad won't be home for a while, so they have time to take the pretty route home through the park. They follow the tree-lined street where heavy-leafed chestnuts bow to the pavement and black-glossed railings proudly point to the skies. Baranina becomes more cheerful and starts to tell Frank all about home. Her house is full of books just for her. Books line the walls and spill from the coffee table. Long-neglected house plants are used as bookends and there's half-drunk cups of tea and spare reading glasses on any remaining horizontal surface. Baranina's Mum and Dad work in publishing and sometimes they bring home books that you can't even find in the bookshops yet.

Baranina has grown up on a steady diet of literature.

'And arrrre you sure that's good for you?' Frank looked at her with wise eyes.

'Mum and Dad say reading is important for a healthy imagination.'

'And do you exercise? Keep active?'

'I have a pogo stick. And I like to climb trees.'

'Hmmm. Verrry good.'

They're nearly at the park when on the street corner she finds a curious-looking table. On it, someone has left a coke bottle, and a half-eaten ham sandwich. On the bottle, tied with a red ribbon is a label that reads: **drink me.**

So she picks up the bottle and unscrews the screwy lid. She's about to have just a tiiiny taste, when...

'Don't, Barrranina. You don't know how long that's been therrrre.'

'Oooh, but look what it says, Frank!'

She places the bottle back down and re-screws the screwy lid to stop flies from dropping in. She has to stand on tippie-toes to see what else is on the table. Beside the ham sandwich is its plastic wrapper which reads: **eat me.** So Baranina reaches over and...

'Same applies, Barrranina. Don't touch it. You don't know wherre it's been.'

'B-b-but...'

'Shall we go into the parrrk and chase the birrds?'

The sandwich is quickly forgotten and they skip into the park

where Frank chases the birds whilst Baranina tries to talk to them.
She spots a little robin sitting by a large, rusty key. She chirps, and
talks, and coaxes and he hops and flits his tail and twitters:

> *I am a*
> *Robin Redbreast,*
> *Who never stops to chat,*
> *Because if I stop and chat*
> *(He says)*
> *You'll know just where I'm at.*
> *And if you know that I'm not home*
> *I know what you'll have for tea*
> *You evil piece of murdering scum,*
> *You'll eat my eggs up, one by one.*

Apparently, Frank's not popular with the birds around here.
The robin flies off to his secret nest and the park is suddenly empty
apart from Baranina, Frank and a strange little boy dressed in delicate skeleton leaves. He isn't shy, and he leaps forward to introduce
himself to Baranina.

'Hello, pretty girl. My name is Peter, what should I call you?'

'Baranina... P-p-peter? I-I-I don't know you from school,
wwhere are you from?'

'Far, far away.'

'F-Far, far away?'

'Yes, take the second star to the right, and go straight on until
morning. I can take you there if you like. It's a beautiful place,
you'd love to see it.'

Frank is growling in a low voice, but Baranina ignores him.
Peter tells her all about his home far, far away in a voice that no girl
can resist. He tells her that he has no parents to look after him and
Baranina feels at once that she is in the presence of a tragedy.

Ignoring Frank's warning looks, she gives the boy a hug.

'I can fly.'

'F-Fly?'

'Yes, want me to teach you?'

Perhaps you have heard of Peter, who hides in the park picking up children who aren't being watched over by their nurses and taking them to a faraway place, where there are treehouses and pirates and everlasting youth.

'I can teach you to fly, Baranina. Why walk home when you might be flying about with me saying funny things to the stars? And, Baranina, there are mermaids.'

'Mermaids with tails?' Baranina's eyes become big and sparkly.

Peter's smiling sweetly and gnashing his little white pearls. He holds out his hand to Baranina. Frank growls louder and louder and flicks his tail like a big angry cat.

'Come with me, Baranina, and you could live forever.'

Baranina hesitates so Peter grabs her arm, hard. All of a sudden, Baranina doesn't feel safe anymore. She stumbles backwards and Peter leaps forward to grab her. So she runs. She runs and runs and the spoon in her lunchbox rattles like a warning drum. She runs until she gets home, and all the way beside her is Frank, leaping at the strange little boy with his big paws and big claws, until eventually Peter is gone, and it's just the two of them by her front gate. Baranina breathes heavily and leans on the wooden fence post.

'Phew,' she says.

'Do you see what I mean about not trusting strrrange creatures you've just met?'

'Come in, I'll make you some food,' Baranina says, without turning around.

The garden is filled with white peony roses, threatening to bloom. Baranina finds the key under an empty plant pot by the door. She unlocks the front door and pushes against its peeling mint-green paint. She steps into the hallway and drops her schoolbag on a pile of books.

She stops to breathe in the smell of dusty paper books and the familiar sweet smell of imagination mingling with the late afternoon sunshine. Frank sees his chance. He's a cat after all and he has an instinct that tells him when to stop playing and when to kill. Her neck is so small the bones crush easily and his teeth grind together in a way that sends a shiver down his spine. She won't be enough, so he'll wait in the kitchen for her Mum and Dad.

THE MICE OF
WINDY NOOK

DEAREST READER, we beg to put before you: The Seamstress of Windy Nook and her Cat.

There is a simple stone cottage in Windy Nook, not far from the sloping fields where slender golden grasses dance in the wild and wicked winds. When the wind bites and the skies turn from grey to slate, we tumble through the grasses and take refuge in the crumbling stone and heather thatched roofs.

We dance along the split oak beams and hide among the teacups. The simple cottage has rooms marked out with neatly-hemmed linen curtains. The kitchen is our favourite area, warm and full of trinkets to hide behind. The hearth is the centre of this cosy scene and on the mantle sit two earthenware hearth spaniels with gold chains and lockets looking down their noses at the simple room. There's no wallpaper, just poor, grubby paintings of faraway landscapes, and a once-pretty blue and red hearth rug that clings to the flagstones by the fireplace.

Here, on her rocking chair, sits the landlady Miss Grace, with eyes as dull as a worm's and ears as sharp as an owl's. As far back as mouselore stretches, Miss Grace has always been there. Quick with a rolling pin, brutal with the coal scuttle, we mice have learned to move as softly as spring drizzle.

One day, the skies lit up with fire and smoke and the earth beneath our paws quivered nervously. Grey clouds fell to earth in soft flakes and our cousins, the mice of The Felling, told us it settled on rooftops like warm snow that choked the lungs.

Miss Grace called it a terrible mining disaster. We saw it as an omen.

Within the week, Miss Grace took in a young lodger, Penny. And with Penny came the daemon of our tale: a mottled brown cat with a big, black tail. Barely out of kittenhood, Cat was confident, calculated, collected.

'Oh, he's a canny cat, Miss Penny,' said Miss Grace, helping Penny with her baskets of thread and cloth, 'I keep a clean hoose, mind ye, but the mice come doon from the hills in autumn. P'haps yor canny cat will larn them.'

'Wor Robert got us 'im.'

Miss Grace looked towards Penny but didn't see the water pooling in her eyes.

'Noo then, ah'll be straight. Ah'm not yer mam so ah'll not stop ye spending time with yer livvor. But ah'll have nae canoodlin' in this hoose. You hear? Wor lad will have tae marry ye and make ye an honest lass if ye's want tae dae that.'

'Oh, but, Miss Grace!' Penny wailed and slumped to the floor, her skirts crumpled around her, 'he's deed, Miss Grace, and all I have left is wor cat and this,' Penny pulled a black satin-covered box from her pocket and opened it for Miss Grace's inspection.

Miss Grace leaned closer and turned her head so that the light hit the contents of the box more favourably. In it was the hollow half-sphere of a glass eye with a sapphire-blue iris.

'Eeeeh, Miss Penny, tha's a bonny engagement ring. Is it sapphire? Topaz? You poor bairn. The pit kilt all our bonny lads and left us lasses with nowt but bonny trinkets.'

Penny peered into Miss Grace's dull eyes, then looked down at the circle of sapphire blue on the glass eye.

'Blue diamond.'

'Eeesh, noo that woudda cost a pretty penny. Hide it well, Miss Penny, an' we'll have nae mare talk aboot bonny stones and deed laddies else we'll be robbed of our trinkets an' our wits. Best tae get on.'

Cat wound his body around Miss Grace's legs and gently head-butted her knee. Miss Grace bent down and scratched Cat's ear. Cat's whiskers unfurled themselves luxuriantly and we knew our quiet time at the stone cottage in Windy Nook was over. There was now more to fear than the coal scuttle.

We became his toys, our screams his music. He'd trace notes on the floor with the blood of our children, careful melodies with a disconcerting tune. He'd wave out the beat of the music with his big, black tail as he mused, composed and tortured.

One evening, the kind of evening with bad weather when all bad things happen, Cat lined the doorstep with the bodies of our sisters, brothers, cousins. He trailed their guts and blood across the threshold in the shape of the time signature and opening bars of Haydn's Symphony No.59.

We scurried to the walls as Penny approached, her thin-fingered hand pressed against her lips.

'Oh, Cat! Why? Why? Death and horror surround us, why'd ye put on such a gruesome display?'

Penny threw Cat out into the pathetic fallacy and went to find the pan and brush.

'Psh! What's this?' Miss Grace said, moving across from the kitchen and turning her head to Penny.

'Cat's kilt twelve tiny mice an' left their poor bodies in bits on the doorstep.'

'An' you threw the poor cat out fer that? He's anly deeing 'is proper job. Fer years those mice have mocked me dull eyes, scampering aboot me kitchen. Cat needs ket, not houying oot!'

Miss Grace opened the door and Cat sprung in lightly with a gale behind him. Miss Grace poured the fatty milk from the top of a fresh bottle into a saucer and Cat lapped it up with pleasure, pausing only occasionally to look around him at the mice that hid in the smallest gaps in the old stone walls.

Penny is a woman of scraps. The people of Windy Nook visit Penny at the cottage with the scraps of their lives; a husband's overalls, a bairn's jacket worn by every three-year-old in Windy Nook, a wedding dress worn by generations. She scraps together her living sewing life back into scraps of fabric with surgical precision.

She saves all the spare bits of fabric from all the gentlemen's coats and all the brides' gowns, nesting them in a heavy, wooden drawer. Soft, cotton, striped, rough, gold, threaded, modern, blue, squares, peach, silk, thick, woollen, heavy, linen, green, fluffy, black. This is a nest we mice love to play in. Accessible only by a splintered back panel (or with the key), the contents of this drawer belong only to us and Penny.

While Penny works, Cat sits blinking in the sun. Penny says Cat is heliotropic because he can find the light even in darkness. Cat sits in the sun for hours, for hours, for hours. Penny follows Cat to the brightest spots in the room. It's the best light for her fine, fine needlework. When the light fades, Miss Grace, Cat and Penny draw around the fire, under the watchful gaze of the hearth spaniels. Penny pulls out Robert's anatomy books and traces her fingers over the delicate illustrations.

She reads how the body is threaded together like a patchwork quilt, each scrap of flesh integral to the whole. She sees how the body is draped in fine threads of red and blue. How a cluster of cells makes a tissue, a cluster of tissues makes an organ. How a cluster of organs make a person, and how delicately put together a man is.

Penny is a self-taught surgeon.

Cat curls in Miss Grace's lap and Miss Grace gently hums as she stares at the frenzied dance of the orange flames. As night draws close, Penny tells stories of her fiancé, but only we and the hearth spaniels listen.

'My Robert was smart. He was the city barber's lad and he was reading to be a surgeon, too. He had eyes like blue diamonds, tha's what I noticed fiorst, when he came tae me fer his jackets repaired. An' then he wanted embroidery work on his cuffs. An' that's when I noticed his lips. Eeh! Like fine, cherry-coloured twist they were, soft like a woman's or a child's. They called him a dandy, but my Robert was a smart man, with a kind face and even though he had but one eye, that was an eye fer details.

'My Robert was gan tae marry me. He anly went doon that mine to ask me dad fer permission. Shudda waited until a Sunday, but my Robert didn't want to wait. He wanted me ootta Windy Nook and living with him in the toon. Nae mare Windy Nook. Nae mare sewin' clays.

'What an unlucky lassie I am. All me world doon a deep, dark pit the day it all went up in flames. Nae blue diamonds, save his glass eye. He didn't want it gummed up with coal dust. Noo I'm here with nowt but surgeon's books, a glass eye and a Cat that likes killin'.'

As late summer burned out into early autumn, the weather became cold and wet, and food became scarce. Our brothers and sisters came down from the hills with golden grasses. We tried to warn them that the stone cottage wasn't what it once was. There were too many of us and as we spilled out of holes in the age-softened stone and scurried from dresser to wardrobe, Cat was always there.

Sometimes, Cat would trap us under cups, to toy with later. He'd pin our tails to the floor and bat us from one paw to the next until we were delirious. He'd then offer up our half-dead bodies to

Miss Grace, who enjoyed the *crunch* of our spines beneath the coal shovel. Once upon a time, we could outrun her, or at least remain so still that her sharp ears and dull eyes could not perceive us. But Cat ensured Miss Grace never missed her target.

After a particularly brutal massacre that ended with Penny crying while gathering decimated, soot-covered bodies that littered the hearth, there came three loud knocks at the door.

Cat arched his back and hissed, and Penny paused, a coal shovel full of tails and paws in her hand.

'Penny for the guy! Penny for the guy! Penny for the guy!'

A gaggle of dirty children with torn clothes stood at the door with a man-sized effigy tied to a small wooden chair. The effigy leaned precariously backwards, the straw-stuffed sleeve hanging on by threads. The children chanted;

> *'Remember, remember, the fifth of November,*
> *Gunpowder treason and plot;*
> *We see no reason why gunpowder treason*
> *Should ever be forgot.'*

Penny quickly covered the coal shovel with a black cloth and rubbed her tears into her cheeks. She looked more closely at the effigy.

'Oh, me days. The state of you lot! Ho'way aw'er here. A've nae pennies, but I'll help ye bairns with wor Guy's arm. Ye'll get nowt with a Guy as tatty-looking as him.'

So, dear readers, we come to the greatest tragedy in our tale. We remember, remember, the fifth of November when the skies lit up with splintered strips of colour and patches of earth glowed orange and hot. And all through the afternoon, all the little boys and little girls rapped on the seamstress' door and called *Penny for the guy, Penny for the guy, Penny for the guy*. They hugged the body of a man who never lived who was the effigy of a man who lived, made of screwed up newspapers sheets and Daddy's cast-off clothes. And the children carried off Penny and Miss Grace to the festivities.

While fires and festivities burned bright and the sky was littered with orange sparks and the smell of smoke and powder permeated the night once more, Cat busied himself in the cottage. Humming Symphony No.59, Cat trapped us under cups. He twitched his tail in time to our screams as he crushed us while we tried to hide beneath the hearth rug.

So few of us remained, so our brave mother led a daring group of young mice to Penny's scrap cloth drawer. But the daemon Cat with his big black tail pounced on the group. He tapped the group back and forth in ¾ time with pink-padded paws. His wet, meaty breath infused our fur with the stench of death.

'Run to the drawer!' Mother cried and as the young mice scurried beneath a flying paw, Mother ran in the opposite direction. Biting hard on the soft flesh of Cat's paw pad, she turned Cat from play to explosive fury. Cat screeched and with a single, extended claw, pinned the skull of Mother to the flagstones.

Of all our brethren, only thirteen of us remained. Six rescued by Mother's sacrifice, five under teacups and one hidden behind each watchful hearth spaniel. Too late, Penny and Miss Grace returned. Peering from the keyhole of the scrap cloth drawer or pressed against the earthenware spaniels' cool glaze, we could not retrieve the bodies of our dead that lay beneath the hearth rug. We could not reach Mother, who lay on the flagstones as if sleeping, a single trail of dark red blood running from her skull and along her nose.

Penny did not make a sound. She scooped up our mother's body and put her gently in her pinafore pocket. Miss Grace brought in the big copper kettle and hooked it above the coals from that morning's fire. Pulling a few twigs from her pinafore pocket that she'd collected from the autumn detritus outside, she teased the fire back to life. She added a fresh, shiny lump of coal to the red and black simmering pile, then dumped her fleshy body into the rocking chair by the fire and crushed the bones of our dead brethren as she rocked back and forth.

Penny gently righted all the teacups until all the trapped mice were freed. Cat looked at Penny and Penny looked at Cat. Then she brought the tea things to the fireside and settled into a hard-backed chair in the dark corner adjacent to the fire so that Miss Grace could not see her well. As they drank their tea, Penny kept her hand in her pinafore pocket and stroked the soft fur of our mother.

When the cold dawn spread its fingers through the thin curtains, Penny was still in the hard-backed chair. We could see that Penny had a plan. An intangible wisp that floated at the back of her head. Wrenching open the drawer, she looked down on us, the survivors.

'Bonny bairns,' she whispered, 'We've all lost too much. Too much. Nae mare. I'll bring us all out of this pit.'

Penny carefully placed Mother into a small square patch of scarlet satin and stitched the bundle together with rough, gold thread so that it looked like a little heart. She stood for a moment with Mother cupped in her seamstress-surgeon hands. A cluster of threads make a piece of material, and a cluster of material and stuffing makes a quilt, with a bit of needlework. To Penny, it seemed simple.

Dawn came and Cat watched with the haughty expression that is his species' trademark as Penny opened up the drawer of scraps and sewed for hours for hours for hours for hours. She worked fast and angrily for two days. Made a thigh from a gentleman's scarf, attached an odd pair of gloves to arms made from scraps of wedding gown and filled the body with blue and red threads. On the third and fourth day, she slowed down, sewing gently and elegantly. She embroidered one diamond blue eye and fixed delicate eyelids made from the inside of a ladies' coat around the glass eye.

Penny took our bodies from the coal shovel and under the

hearth rug. She made little parcels in the shapes she saw in Robert's anatomy books. When the effigy began to take human form, Penny carried him to her bed and pulled the grey linen curtain around him so that Miss Grace could not see our guy.

When Penny placed Mother in her heart-shaped satin casket into the chest of the man, we saw the cloth parcels begin to pulse and quiver. Mother's parcel began to beat in ¾ time. We climbed into the chest and wound the red and blue threads tighter, closing up gaps and adjusting the placement of each organ. We felt the man warming up. He smelt like the scrap cloth draw, of many humans, of many mice, of dust and a little bit of linseed oil.

Penny slow, steadily, strongly, sewed up the sternum and we, the remaining mice of Windy Nook, nestled deeper into the man. Our blood became his blood. Our life force became his and he came into being. The guy moved and murmured softly, gently on the bed. He struggled to inhale life-giving air through his blanket-stitch-hemmed nose.

'Oh, oh, he'll suffocate. We need a mouth. An' ah need the fine, cherry-coloured twist tae dae it," breathed Penny, scurrying through baskets and drawers in search of thread with her fine-fingered hands. She gripped the guy's hand and we warmed up, breathed slower, more easily, in her embrace.

'Hush, hush, now. Breathe easy, bonny laddie. You must have lips made from the finest cherry-coloured twist. And ah knaa just where tae get it.'

Penny kissed her guy where the lips would be and we calmed, settled, nestled down, ready for our final incarnation. She took some coins from the pouch she hid in her sewing box and left the cottage.

The sun shifted in the sky and our skin softened in the dappled afternoon sunshine. We felt warm, alive, and we enjoyed the scent of cloth drying and warming in the sun. It reminded us of the fields of Windy Nook in summer when we were all alive and we'd slip through the tall, golden grasses and howling winds and into the yard when Miss Grace dried her clothes. But, dear readers, it was nearing winter and the sun did not last. Cold and darkness came over us and with it a new smell. The smell of hot, meaty breath.

Cat arched his back and hissed at the guy lying on Penny's bed. He paused, then sprung neatly onto the foot of the bed and sniffed at our toes. Dear reader, we could feel. We could all feel the gentle brush of Cat's whiskers on our naked leg. We felt his wet nose as he sniffed our thigh and worked his way alongside our body. We felt the press of a paw on our chest and smelled his horrible breath as he neared our nose. And with our diamond blue eyes, we saw our chance. Pulling a thousand red and blue threads and kneading a hundred muscles made from wool and cotton and linen, our guy sat up and punched Cat to the floor.

Cat screamed two discordant notes and sprang from the bed to the floor, tearing down the curtain.

'Esh, now, what's this,' cried Miss Grace from the kitchen. We heard her shuffle across the worn flagstones and, still sitting upright, Guy turned his head to look at her. Miss Grace only saw the glint of one glass eye.

'Who's that? Who are ye?' Miss Grace's dull eyes narrowed in the growing darkness. Hearing no reply, she moved quickly back to the fireplace where she grabbed the coal shovel and lit a candle from the fire she'd just nurtured to life.

'Who are ye? Talk quickly, noo. The blacksmith lives right across the road, but half the toon will hear me yell if yer here tae cause bother.'

With no mouth, we could not make a sound, so we pulled threads and twisted cotton, extending our guy's hand with an open palm. Miss Grace edged closer, holding the candle out in front of her. All she could see was one bright-blue glass eye catching the candle's light and the heavy, broad-shouldered shape of a man. Lowering the coal shovel, her face changed, her wrinkles relaxing back into the folds of her skin to form a softer expression.

'Are ye...' she began, but Cat cut her short. Freeing himself from the linen curtains on the floor, he screamed again and leapt, claws outstretched, to Miss Grace's legs. She tumbled and hit the floor with a thud and a groan.

We began to breathe more quickly, losing control of our rhythm and recoiling as our skin began to twitch and crawl. We remember, remember the mining disaster. The smell of burning. The crack and pop of orange flames drinking in all of the air, all of the clear air and filling our lungs with sticky, thick smoke. Our legs were too heavy to move, our thinking dimmed by the smoke.

'Get oot! Get oot!' Miss Grace screamed, stumbling to the kitchen and throwing open the door. The fire took a deep breath, sucking in the air that rushed in from the open door. Through bars of orange flame, we saw Cat's big black tail bob out of the door at the heels of Miss Grace. And Penny, our two different eyes saw Penny, the hems of her dress and apron sweeping up flames as she dashed towards us.

We remember screams and cries, but there is no more. Dear readers, read on. We beg to put before you the Tale of Penny and her Guy. But there is no more, except to say, on a wild and wicked night, go down to the sloping fields of Windy Nook where golden grasses dance. Listen carefully and you might hear us singing, hand in hand, cherry-coloured lips to flesh as soft as ash at last.

THE GIRL IN THE PIED DRESS

I'M CHOKING on the smoke. The heat presses against me like a thick blanket. The skin on my legs is starting to peel and I think the pain might make me vomit, though there's nothing in my stomach to make me vomit. They did not give me food in the prison.

I try to breathe more deeply. They're watching me, tied here naked, cloaked only in flames and smoke. They want me to scream. They want to see me writhe. The smoke makes me cough, but I try to inhale as much of it as I can. A wise woman once told me it's not the fire that kills, it is the smoke. And I desperately want to be dead before the flames reach beyond my knees.

My feet feel wet. I think it is because the flesh has burned off, leaving blood and sinew exposed. I want to die before the flames reach my breast tissue. I can't stop thinking about how bad the pain will become when the flames reach my more delicate flesh. My feet have done well – they have endured a lot. They are a willing sacrifice.

Three children are in the turret with rocks in their hands. They're the only children here. They throw the rocks at me and the crowd cheers. A light breeze twists and teases the smoke and stokes the flames. I take another lung-full of smoke and through a momentary gap in the smoke's screen, I see the Laird. His green eyes are locked on mine as others around him dance and chatter like it is fete day and I am just a doll for their entertainment. In the prison, he told me watching the prisoners burn, especially the women prisoners, made him hard. I am the first execution in almost a decade and I feel a flash of anger, of embarrassment, for being here naked and in pain for his sick entertainment. But I don't want to die with vengeance and hate on my mind. That is not the way of a warrior.

I'm running through the woods. The soft yellow shimmer of the hazelnut catkins salutes us as we pass and we weave through the slender silver birch trees that are gathered in protective groups. I'm looking out for the alder trees, because I know we'll be closer to the water when we see them. The water is important to me, it's the outer boundary of everything I have known. We will be safe when we cross it.

Harriet stumbles and I reach for her, righting her.

'Don't fall and hurt yourself, not here,' I say. She squeezes my hand.

She wears black with a white, piped collar. I'm wearing my multi-coloured dress, the one Mamma and I made with scrap material from the performers' tent. Harriett and I make an odd-looking pair but we know our hearts skip to the same beat. We know what we're doing is right.

Wet eyes glimmer from the darkness of the woods. They look to us, the eldest of the town's surviving children, to lead them somewhere better.

I force a smile, 'Let's keep going, we'll be at the water soon,' I say and wave my hands to hurry them.

I could be chasing them down one of the dusty village lanes, shooing them and their games away from damp sheets on the line.

A young boy with ginger curls and a loose-fitting ochre shirt grins at me and skips ahead. He seems so young, so oblivious to what we are doing, I wonder for a moment if what we're doing is right. I turn back and recognise his sister, Olivia, by her red ringleted hair. She's the daughter of musicians too. Her mother is a dancer and her father is a drummer, renowned for his heart-rousing rhythms. He'd play at every celebration, every call to arms. But he wasn't at our protest and when I asked Olivia why she'd told me her parents were gone too.

Olivia is carrying a baby, about six months old. The baby is chewing on a loose ringlet of hair. Olivia tries to shuffle the baby higher into her arms, but the baby's long white dress is tangled over one arm.

'Here, let me take him for a while,' I say and cradle the baby's head as we break into a half-run again.

I surge ahead and lead the group, quietly humming a tune that barely carries above the rustle of leaves and the sigh of the wind swimming through the upper branches. The dancing, dappled light on the woodland floor makes me feel as though we're under-water and I'm encouraged. We must be getting there. Harriet herds the children from the back, keeping an eye out for young stragglers and the Beauderre Girls.

Something's always been wrong with the Beauderre Girls – Stephanie is blind, Rosalie is lame, Charlotte is deaf and they don't hold hope in their hearts as other children do. Harriett says it's not their fault they're the Laird's children. Harriet says dark things happen to all children in the Laird's castle, no matter their lineage, and I'm reminded of my recurring nightmares of what might happen there.

I think of all the other children who turned sixteen in the luna month of the summer solstice. The children who were taken to the castle – the boys to the walls, to be trained up and sent to foreign wars. The girls into the inner chambers, to serve the laird in his dark chateaux. I'm reminded of the smell of burning flesh, almost ten years ago today, when they burned the Beauderre's aunt for trying to take the girls away.

We promised all the children we'd look out for each other so that the future is better than today. We promised that we'd all go. No one would be left behind. No one would have to go to the castle when they turned sixteen. We'd build a new town deep in the woods and together, we'd build a better society.

But I still wasn't sure about bringing the Beauderre Girls. Harriett reminded me there was a place for everyone in our new world: rich or poor, or blind, or lame, or deaf. She reminded me of the promise I'd made to my mother. Harriet is less vengeful than me. She's always been that way. Moderate, modest, measured.

'Vengeance is not the way of the warrior,' she told me she'd read this in a book.

I was ashamed. I'm the adventurous one, the bold one, the warrior. So, it had been me who crept to the Laird's chateaux to wake the Beauderre Girls early that morning to tell them that today was the day we were leaving for a new, faraway land. I'd gathered hazelnuts from the woodland and threw them into the turret window I'd seen them hiding in. And all morning they had surprised me. They'd played on each other's superior faculties to get out of the castle and guide each other through the dark woodlands. They'd kept up with the group.

Charlotte, the eldest sister, walked ahead and picked a smooth path for Rosalie, who sang softly so that Stephanie, the youngest, could follow her sound.

Stephanie added her own sweet harmony to the tune as she went, and it kept our spirits up. She has a taste for sound and music. She can hear fear and love. And she has a singing voice that could lure the songbirds.

I noticed that Rosalie's slowness has taught her to notice things, details that others miss in their hurry to race through life. It was Rosalie who'd made the rope from bedsheets strong enough to lower each girl down from the turret in the cool morning light.

Charlotte is quick, strong and nimble. She could be a dancer – or a warrior. The other children from the castle say she can throw a hazelnut with such precision and force, it can knock a man out. I don't want to know why she has nurtured this skill. But I am impressed nonetheless.

I know now that I was wrong to judge the Beauderre Girls. Perhaps they've overcome more than any of us.

'Why hadn't you escaped before?' I'd asked, as we'd made our way to meet the other children at the edge of the woodlands.

'Who would lead us? Where would we go? Together, we are stronger,' Charlotte said and hugged me.

Alder trees suddenly appear in front of us. Their knotted roots stretch out, desperate to dip their toes in the water. Curiously, I see the river before I hear it.

'Wait,' I say to Olivia's brother. He toys with the edges of his ochre shirt.

I unlace my boots, place them to one side and step confidently into the river, pushing the baby higher onto my shoulder. My footsteps become slow and steady and as the river gets deeper the colours of my dress become richer. I reach the other side and look at the waterline on my dress. It's up to my navel and I know the river will be too deep for the younger children. We'll have to work together.

Leaving the baby nestled in alder roots on the other side, I wade back over and get the children to form a chain across the river, holding hands and dragging the smallest children through the water.

The current is not too strong, but it is enough to worry some of the children. Harriet and I stand waist-deep in the water, steading everyone and helping them across.

Finally on the other side, I realise I've left my boots on the wrong side of the river. Olivia picks up her baby brother and grasps the hand of the boy in the ochre shirt.

'Thanks,' she says, 'get your boots, we'll keep everyone

moving,' and she strides confidently over the tangled alder roots. I admire the way she suddenly looks older, stronger, and watch her shape smoulder into a shadowy silhouette in the broken woodland light. I'm turning back to face the river when a scream breaks out above the water's rush.

'RUN!'

And we turn and run. I don't know why we are running. A dark feeling more than a dark thing. But I know we must. We scatter through the trees and it's hard to keep track of everyone.

Something sharp rips open the soft skin on the arch of my foot. I leap a few steps, then turn. My boots are by the river, still.

'Are you okay?' Harriett grabs my arm, pulling me towards the dark shade of two birch trees that have grown up close together.

Harriett cleans my foot and binds her russet-red handkerchief around it.

'The Girls,' I whisper, 'where are the Beauderres?' Harriett covers her mouth and widens her eyes.

'We've got to keep going. You keep going, I'll find them. We'll catch up,' I look at Harriett, who looks at the children between the trees. She squeezes my hand and nods, just once.

I run on the balls of my feet until I reach the river, where we'd heard the strange scream that set us all off running. We're not strong enough to fight what's back in our home town, that's why we choose to run, for now. Running towards something better for us all. We are too young to go backward, to fight the past. We must go forwards.

My boots are propped up between the alder roots on the other side, pointing in the direction we're headed. I wade across and put them on, angry at myself for taking them off. A warrior should not be afraid of wet boots. I can't hear or see anything to be afraid of, but heading back towards the town makes me feel uneasy. The river was further than any of us had ever been before. It felt important to cross it.

I slip quietly from tree to tree, wincing when I feel the cut on my foot stretch and split further. Harriett's binding is still tight around it. I try to stay sharp, attentive to my surroundings. Birds clap their wings and scratch and twitch in the trees. The skin on my face prickles. The leaves smell damp and dirty, like something unpleasant has been uncovered.

I'm about a third of the way back to town when a green-clad hazelnut drops in front of me. I look up and they're there: Stephanie and Charlotte are, anyway. Rosalie is curled beneath two large intertwining roots.

'Shhh, they're close. They're really, really close. With the dogs. They were waiting for us at the river, they saw us crossing, but they were too far downstream to catch you. We tried to lead them away. Did you not get away?' Rosalie says.

'The others did. I came back for you,' I whisper back.

'You shouldn't have. They'll get you. They'll get you for leading the children away.'

She's crying silently. The forest has gone quiet too. Only the strange dead-damp-leaf smell hangs in the air. I lift her into the tree, high enough so that her sisters can catch her arms and pull her up. There's a deep, guttural sound from behind me. I look but see nothing, so I start to climb the tree. The bark feels rough under my hands, but I like how steady, how secure the tree feels.

I'm not far off the ground when the hunting dog catches my ankles in its jaw. I can't shake it off. I can't. A second hunting dog begins to circle the tree, making a low, guttural growl. I let my hands slide from the branches and try to pull myself away from the tree where the Beauderres are hiding. I manage to throw them a look, one I hope says: keep hiding, then go, go and cross the river.

But it's no good. The dogs belong to the Beauderres' eldest brother, Oswyn. The dogs know the girls and they know they're up there. Oswyn is there soon after the dogs, followed by some of the townsmen and the Laird.

'You. Of course it would be you. Think you could steal all the children in the town and get away with it? Don't you know what the punishment is for child kidnapping? Don't you know what we do to women like you? Where are the other children?'

'Gone. They've all gone,' I say, but I don't think anyone can hear me. They're climbing up and dragging the Beauderre girls down from the tree.

'We chose to go, we chose to go!' shouts Rosalie, but she knows better than anyone what will happen to me. She's old enough to remember what happened to her aunty.

I'm old enough to know the consequences of my actions.

I'm marching through the streets to the castle. Tomorrow, I'll be sixteen. Harriett holds my hand tightly. We shout and sing and wave colourful flags, which we made from the scraps of the performers' tent. I'm wearing a colourful dress, striped with all the colours you could imagine.

My Mamma is the famous chalumeaux player, the dress is hers, the mark of a musician. I'm old enough now to fit into her clothes, so I wear them in protest, as a reminder. She disappeared two weeks ago.

That morning, a fortnight ago, I woke from a bad dream. I couldn't see clearly, my eyes and mind fogged with the thick smoke of the nightmare. I blinked and rubbed my eyes. I clutched my chest and felt my heart beating so quickly I thought it might pop out.

My Mamma shouted from the kitchen.

'Get up! Get ready! I need you out here!'

We slept in a shared room, my Mamma and me. I saw her bed was made and that the room had a warm, mid-morning glow. I folded back the blankets and leaned on the door frame. The earth felt warm beneath my feet.

'What are you doing? I need your help,' Mamma said, then turned to look at me, 'oh, oh no... another nightmare?'

I rubbed my eyes and nodded my head. The weight of my

dream was heavy on me. She grabbed my shoulders and pressed her warm thumbs into my shoulder blades.

'You're not going to that castle. Do you hear me? The day you turn sixteen, you'll be right here with me, hanging the sheets, scrubbing the copper and feeding the chickens. Do you hear? I will not let them take you to the castle.'

Her smile punctured dimples in her cheeks and her chestnut hair escaped in whisps from her plait. This is how I remember her.

'Well, take your time. Go get ready. And hurry up, I need you now. I have a plan and I'd like your help,' she turned back to the reams of coloured cloth on the workbench.

I pulled off my nightgown and shuffled to the pump in the backyard, gasping as the cold water hit my neck. But it washed off the dark cloud of my dream and I felt renewed. I watched the water, clouded with soap, swirl down the drain and I imagined my worries swirling away with it.

Mamma told me the plan – a colourful protest, with all the musicians and players singing and all the people dancing. They'd play through the village, they'd play through the fields and over the hills to the castle walls, with Mamma and her chalumeaux leading the way. They'd play over the bridge and to the castle keep and they'd sing so loudly the Laird and all his men could not ignore their cries and songs:

Where, oh where, do our flowers go?
Where, oh where, do our flowers go?
Oh, not to the meadows,
To dance in the breeze.
Not to the woodlands,
To sleep beneath the trees.

Where, oh where, do our flowers go?
Where, oh where, do our flowers go?

Not into the fields,
To grow in the sunlight,
Not reaching for dawn,
Growing, blooming bright.

Where, oh where, do our flowers go?
Where, oh where, do our flowers go?
Into the night, our flowers go
Wrapped in stone walls,
To wilt in darkness,
Trapped in the Laird's chateaux,
To wallow in his sickness.

No more, no more, will our flowers grow,
No more, no more, will our flowers go.

We hummed the tune as we worked, sewing colourful flags and clothes and banners for all the villagers. Mamma would not let me protest with her and she sent me with the other almost-sixteen-year-olds into the woodlands.

I met Harriet by an old oak tree on the edge of the village. From its heavy boughs, we could see everything from the blacksmith's forge at the fringe of the village to the castle keep that stands on the mound in the centre of town. We looked out over the black and white wooden cottages with their thatched roofs and winding alleyways that give way to the castle's sharp-cornered stone walls and pointed turrets.

Harriett and I often find privacy behind the woodland trees. We believe the moss-tinged bark absorbs our secrets and the low branches reach out to us in an embrace. Promising something better, loftier. Something closer to the heavens.

We nestled in the embrace of the large oak and held hands.

We promised each other that whatever happened, we'd stay together. Even if we had to go to the castle. Then we waited as dusk swallowed the daylight and the streets glowed orange with torches. The coloured flags lost their colour, but not their vibrancy in the dark. That sweet tune could be heard long into the night and together, we hummed it as we fell asleep.

Mamma did not return that night. But I am not alone. Many of the other parents and protesters did not return, either.

The Laird says Mamma and the others just want notoriety. More fame, more money. That they're doing it for the attention, to bring him down. The Laird says Mamma and the others who spoke out ran away because they're guilty of lying and this town doesn't suffer liars.

He said he'd take us all in, Harriet and I, and the other boys and girls who would turn sixteen in the month of the summer solstice. And he said he'd take the other children of the protesters too. He said it was the best thing for us. Those too young to work would be looked after by his church until they were old enough to enter the castle. So I took my Mamma's colourful clothes and banners and today, I marched out into the streets singing.

As I sang, they all came out. All of the children of the missing protesters, other young parents with their babies and even some of the older townspeople. Harriett slipped her gentle hand into mine and together we led the march and song.

Where, oh where, do our flowers go?
Where, oh where, do our flowers go?

So here we are. All singing together at the feet of the castle's rough walls. The streets are full with people, with song and coloured rags again. We plan to sing and dance until a new Laird is selected. The day is cloudy but the air smells sweet. There's the sound of drums, tambourines and chalumeaux – though no one plays it quite so well as my Mamma.

The castle peers down at us. Movement catches my eye. The Laird's men appear at the guardhouse windows with crossbows at their shoulders. Daggers rattle at belts as a steady chainmail-clad line of the Laird's men march out through a small door in the castle walls. The crowds quieten to a murmur. Harriett squeezes my hand.

I notice the Laird's children, the Beauderre Girls, watching from a turret. Three young sisters, one blind, one lame, one deaf.

'Look,' I point them out to Harriett and she reminds me of their aunty, the witch. She tried to kidnap the Beauderre Girls, but she was caught and burned at the stake. Harriett and I weren't old enough to go, but as Harriett reminds me of her story it comes back to me: the smell of burned fat and flesh that lingered in the streets for days afterwards. I feel sick. My eyes blur and smoke from a torch I cannot see catches in my throat. I look around. Our voices are too loud. Our clothes too vibrant.

'I think we should go to the woodlands, now, to sleep beneath the trees. We'll go until we find the meadows, where we can dance in the breeze. Harriett, oh, we should go away from the castle, not to it! There will be no change while that rat is in his tower.' Harriett nods and looks at me. I smooth down the folds of my pied dress.

I gulp another thick mouthful of smoke. The grey clouds and orange flames dance frenetically around me. The shimmering heat makes the scene around me blurry. I want to rub my eyes. They sting.

The Laird moves forward to throw another oak branch onto the fire. It does nothing to add to the flames, but the crowd cheers anyway and I see the Laird looking at my breasts. He massages his crotch and twists his face as he rolls phlegm around his mouth then spits it at my feet.

I look down. I cannot see my feet. A layer of skin hangs from my right leg and it reminds me of the peeling bark of the birch tree. My stomach turns and I want to vomit, but my stomach is empty. My throat is too hot and dry.

A rock strikes me on my chin. It is nothing compared to the pain of the burns and, with my failing mind, this makes me realise: the children throwing the rocks are the Beauderre Girls. The crowd is cheering again. The crowd thinks the girls are taunting me, but now I realise: they're trying to kill me before the flames do.

The flesh on my wrists rips as I twist around to face the girls. The crowd sees my struggle and cheers again. Our tune comes to my mind and I start to sing, but no sound comes out. It does not matter. I want to die with our song on my lips. That is the way of a warrior.

Where, oh where, do our flowers go?
Where, oh where, do our flowers go?
Oh, not to the meadows, to dance in the breeze.
Not to the woodlands, to sleep beneath the trees.

I breathe as deeply as I can and I see a blurry Charlotte. Charlotte, who is so strong she can knock a man out with a hazelnut. I see her, arm raised, a large rock flying from her hand.

ACKNOWLEDGEMENTS

Thank you to everyone who has supported me over the years while I have cried, sweated and whinged over this collection. I'm overwhelmed by the support I've had in writing these stories and in sharing them with the world. To you, dear reader, thank you for picking up my short story collection and giving it a read. I hope you've enjoyed it.

This collection was completed with the invaluable help of Creative New Zealand and the New Zealand Society of Authors Te Puni Kaituhi O Aotearoa (PEN NZ Inc), through the NZSA Mentor Programme 2021. Thanks especially to Majella Cullinane, my wonderful mentor.

Thanks to Liz Breslin for your careful reading and suggestions. I couldn't have done it without you!

Thank you to Sara Litchfield for being a constant source of inspiration, random chit-chat and mad ideas.

To Stuart Macdonald, thank you for rescuing my design efforts!

A variation of The Cuckoo was shortlisted for the Manchester Fiction Prize (2011).

Great Grandmother's Stories was first published in 1964 Magazine (2022) and was first performed by Remarkable Theatre in 2019.

ABOUT THE AUTHOR

B. G. Rogers is a short story writer and poet from Newcastle-Upon-Tyne (UK). She currently lives in Queenstown, Aotearoa New Zealand with a ginormous house rabbit called Oscar Wilde.

Her work has been published internationally and commended by Aesthetica Magazine, shortlisted for the Manchester Fiction Prize and longlisted in the New Zealand Flash Fiction Day competition.

She's a founding trustee of the Queenstown Writers Festival and a member and organiser of the Queenstown Creative Writing Group. *Kaleidoscopes in the Dark* is her first short story collection.

Find out more at bgrogers.com/creative-fiction

Rabbiting On

Kit and Posy hope that these'll
Find some favour with The Weasel;
Also Stephen (call him King).
May these pics and poems bring
Joy to Anna J and Sarah,
Who'll be kind enough to share a
Look at then with Caroline
(Pics by Posy, poems mine).
Then there's Becky and her pal,
The boy the bruisers call Big Al.
To them and all the rest who like
With sawn-off walking sticks to strike
A tennis ball a mighty way
On that fine golf-course, Booby's Bay,
We dedicate the book upon
Whose cover you'll read RABBITING ON . . . .

Kit Wright is far too tall and likes poems, beer, cricket
and Posy Simmonds.

Posy Simmonds likes drawing, Kit's jokes, singing in the
bath and wine gums.

Other poetry titles in Lions and Young Lions

Toughie Toffee *David Orme* (ed)
Salford Road *Gareth Owen*
Song of the City *Gareth Owen*
Hairy Tales and Nursery Crimes *Michael Rosen*
The Hypnotiser *Michael Rosen*
Mind Your Own Business *Michael Rosen*
When Did You Last Wash Your Feet? *Michael Rosen*
Out of the Blue *Fiona Waters* (ed)
A Children's Zoo *Julia Watson* (ed)
The Lions Book of Young Verse *Julia Watson* (ed)

Rabbiting On

and Other Poems

by Kit Wright

Illustrations by Posy Simmonds

First published in Great Britain in Lions 1978
Eleventh impression June 1991

Lions is an imprint of
the Children's Division, part of
HarperCollins Publishers Ltd,
77–85 Fulham Palace Road,
Hammersmith, London W6 8JB

ISBN 0 00 671342-4

Printed and bound in Great Britain by
HarperCollins Book Manufacturing, Glasgow

Contents

Rabbiting On

Where did you go?
Oh . . . nowhere much.

What did you see?
Oh . . . rabbits and such.

Rabbits? What else?
Oh . . . a rabbit hutch.

What sort of rabbits?
What sort? Oh . . . small.

What sort of hutch?
Just a hutch, that's all.

But what did it look like?
Like a rabbit hutch.

Well, what was in it?
Small rabbits and such.

I worried about you
While you were gone.

*Why don't you stop
Rabbiting on?*

Me

My Mum is on a diet,
My Dad is on the booze,
My Gran's out playing Bingo
And she was born to lose.

My brother's stripped his motorbike
Although it's bound to rain.
My sister's playing Elton John
Over and over again.

What a dim old family!
What a dreary lot!
Sometimes I think that I'm the only
Superstar they've got.

Whisper Whisper

whisper whisper
whisper whisper
goes my sister
down the phone

whisper whisper
go the becch leaves
breathing in the
wind alone

whisper whisper
whisper whisper
slips the river
on the stone

whisper whisper
go my parents
when they whisper
on their own

I don't mind the
whisper whisper
whisper whisper
it's a tune

sometimes though
I wish the whisper
whisperings would
shut up soon

The Wicked Singers

And have you been out carol singing,
Collecting for the Old Folk's Dinner?

Oh yes indeed, oh yes indeed.

And did you sing all the Christmas numbers,
Every one a winner?

Oh yes indeed, oh yes indeed.

Good King Wenceslas, and Hark
The Herald Angels Sing?

Oh yes indeed, oh yes indeed.

And did you sing them loud and clear
And make the night sky ring?

Oh yes indeed, oh yes indeed.

And did you count up all the money?
Was it quite a lot?

Oh yes indeed, oh yes indeed.

And did you give it all to the Vicar,
Everything you'd got?

Certainly not, certainly not.

My Party

My parents said I could have a party
And that's just what I did.

Dad said, "Who had you thought of inviting?"
I told him. He said, "Well, you'd better start writing,"
And that's just what I did

To:

Phyllis Willis, Horace Morris,
Nancy, Clancy, Bert and Gert Sturt,
Dick and Mick and Nick Crick,
Ron, Don, John,
Dolly, Molly, Polly—
Neil Peel—
And my dear old friend, Dave Dirt.

I wrote, "Come along, I'm having a party,"
And that's just what they did.

They all arrived with huge appetites
As Dad and I were fixing the lights.
I said, "Help yourself to the drinks and bites!"
And that's just what they did,
All of them:

Phyllis Willis, Horace Morris,
Nancy, Clancy, Bert and Gert Sturt,
Dick and Mick and Nick Crick,
Ron, Don, John,
Dolly, Molly, Polly-
Neil Peel—
And my dear old friend, Dave Dirt.

Now, I had a good time and as far as I could tell,
The party seemed to go pretty well—
Yes, that's just what it did.

Then Dad said, "Come on, just for fun,
Let's have a *turn* from everyone!"
And a turn's just what they did,

All of them:

Phyllis Willis, Horace Morris,
Nancy, Clancy, Bert and Gert Sturt,
Dick and Mick and Nick Crick,
Ron, Don, John,
Dolly, Molly, Polly—
Neil Peel—
And my dear old friend, Dave Dirt.

AND THIS IS WHAT THEY DID:

Phyllis and Clancy
And Horace and Nancy
Did a song and dance number
That was really fancy—

Dolly, Molly, Polly,
Ron, Don and John
Performed a play
That went on and on and on—

Gert and Bert Sturt,
Sister and brother,
Did an imitation of
Each other.

(Gert Sturt put on Bert Sturt's shirt
And Bert Sturt put on Gert Sturt's skirt.)

Neil Peel
All on his own
Danced an eightsome reel.

Dick and Mick
And Nicholas Crick
Did a most *ingenious*
Conjuring trick

And my dear old friend, Dave Dirt,
Was terribly sick
All over the flowers.
We cleaned it up.
It took *hours.*

But as Dad said, giving a party's not easy.
You really
Have to
Stick at it.
I agree. And if Dave gives a party
I'm certainly
Going to be
Sick at it.

Doris

There was a young lady called Doris
Who had a twin sister called Chloris,
    One brother called Maurice,
    Another called Norris
And two more called Horace and Boris.

Now Doris was quite fond of Chloris
And she didn't mind Maurice or Norris
    But she hated Horace
    And Horace loathed Boris

And Horace, Boris, Maurice, Norris
and Chloris couldn't take Doris *at
any price at all.*

Give Up Slimming, Mum

My Mum
is short
and plump
and pretty
and I wish
she'd give up
slimming.

So does Dad.

Her cooking's
delicious—
you can't
beat it—
but you really can
hardly bear
to eat it—
the way she sits
with her eyes
brimming,
watching you
polish off
the spuds
and trimmings
while she
has nothing
herself but a small
thin dry
diet biscuit:
that's all.

My Mum
is short
and plump
and pretty
and I wish
she'd give up
slimming.

So does Dad.

She says she
looks as though
someone had
sat on her—
BUT WE LIKE MUM
WITH A BIT
OF FAT ON HER!

Dad and the Cat and the Tree

This morning a cat got
Stuck in our tree.
Dad said, "Right, just
Leave it to me."

The tree was wobbly,
The tree was tall.
Mum said, "For goodness'
Sake don't fall!"

"Fall?" scoffed Dad,
"A climber like me?
Child's play, this is!
You wait and see."

He got out the ladder
From the garden shed.
It slipped. He landed
In the flower bed.

"Never mind", said Dad,
Brushing the dirt
Off his hair and his face
And his trousers and his shirt,

"We'll try Plan B. Stand
Out of the way!"
Mum said, "Don't fall
Again, O.K.?"

"Fall again?" said Dad.
"Funny joke!"
Then he swung himself up
On a branch. It broke.

Dad landed *wallop*
Back on the deck.
Mum said, "Stop it,
You'll break your neck!"

"Rubbish!" said Dad.
"Now we'll try Plan C.
Easy as winking
To a climber like me!"

Then he climbed up high
On the garden wall.
Guess what?
He *didn't fall*!

He gave a great leap
And he landed flat
In the crook of the tree-trunk—
Right on the cat!

The cat gave a yell
And sprang to the ground,
Pleased as Punch to be
Safe and sound.

So it's smiling and smirking,
Smug as can be,
But poor old Dad's
Still

Stuck
Up
The
Tree!

Grandad

Grandad's dead
And I'm sorry about that.

He'd a huge black overcoat.
He felt proud in it.
You could have hidden
A football crowd in it.
Far too big—
It was a lousy fit
But Grandad didn't
Mind a bit.
He wore it all winter
With a squashed black hat.

Now he's dead
And I'm sorry about that.

He'd got twelve stories.
I'd heard every one of them
Hundreds of times
But that was the fun of them:
You knew what was coming
So you could join in.
He'd got big hands
And brown, grooved skin
And when he laughed
It knocked you flat.

Now he's dead
And I'm sorry about that.

My Dad, Your Dad

My dad's fatter than your dad,
Yes, my dad's fatter than yours:
If he eats any more he won't fit in the house,
He'll have to live out of doors.

Yes, but my dad's balder than your dad,
My dad's balder, O.K.,
He's only got two hairs left on his head
And both are turning grey.

Ah, but my dad's thicker than your dad,
My dad's thicker, all right.
He has to look at his watch to see
If it's noon or the middle of the night.

Yes, but my dad's more boring than your dad.
If he ever starts counting sheep
When he can't get to sleep at night, he finds
It's the sheep that go to sleep.

But my dad doesn't mind your dad.
Mine quite likes yours too.
I suppose they don't always think much of US!
That's true, I suppose, that's true.

Did You Ever!

Did you ever
Meet an old man in a sky-blue overcoat?
Yes? Well, so did I.

Hat on his head,
Hands on his knees,
Beard on his face,
Pipe in his mouth
And a look in his eye
That said:
"I may not be too clever, folks,
But goodness knows, I try!"

You met him and so did I.

Did you ever
Meet an old woman in a sharkskin waistcoat?
Yes? Well, so did I.

    Cap on her head,
    Freckles on her knees,
    Grin on her face,
    Twig in her mouth
    And a look in her eye
    That said:
    "I'm feeling frisky as a two-week kitten,
    Somebody tell me why!"

You met her and so did I.

Did you ever
Meet an old dog in velvet trousers?
Never? Neither did I.

Swaybacks in the Springtime

Two old horses, piebald swaybacks,
Mooching down by the chestnut trees:
Sharing a field in spring, though these
Are the winter days of their lives.

Two old horses, put out to grass here,
Suddenly break, frisk into a run
And their tough manes gleam in the rising sun
In the winter days of their lives.

Sergeant Brown's Parrot

Many policemen wear upon their shoulders
Cunning little radios. To pass away the time
They talk about the traffic to them, listen to the news,
And it helps them to Keep Down Crime.

But Sergeant Brown, he wears upon his shoulder
A tall green parrot as he's walking up and down
And all the parrot says is "Who's-a-pretty-boy-then?"
"I am," says Sergeant Brown.

Sergeant Brown's Parrot's Girl-Friend

Sergeant Brown's parrot's girl-friend
Squawked to herself in a hickory tree:
"They say my parrot boy's no good,
They say he's lousy as can be.
　　They put him down
　　In every way
　　But what I say
Is: Good enough for Sergeant Brown
　　Is good enough for me!"

That splendid Sergeant Brown
That strides about the town!

So Sergeant Brown's parrot's girl-friend
Flew till she came where Sergeant Brown,
Her tall green lover on his shoulder,
Was pacing grandly up and down.
    She whispered low
    In her lover's ear:
    "It's me, my dear.
Tell me, truly, who's-a-pretty-girl-then?"
    "I am," said Sergeant Brown.

That frightful Sergeant Brown
That strides about the town!

Sergeant Brown's Parrot and Sir Robert Mark

Sir Robert Mark, Police Commissioner,
Heard of a Sergeant who had dared to position a

Parrot on his shoulder. "A what?" he said.
"PARROT. TALL. GREEN. ALONGSIDE HIS HEAD.

SMART. WELL-SPOKEN. A BIRD OF BREEDING.
PROCEEDS WHEREVER THE SERGEANT'S PROCEEDING."

The report was delivered at a Working Luncheon.
Sir Robert banged his plate with his silver truncheon.

The plate broke in half. No-one dared to laugh.
"Bring this man in!" he roared to his staff.

The Sergeant was working on a dog theft case,
Sitting at his desk with his parrot in place.

"Come on, Brown!" they yelled, "better make it snappy—
Sir Robert Mark wants you and he isn't too happy!"

So off went the Sergeant and the parrot and the rest of them,
Arrived where Sir Robert was scoffing with the best of them.

Sergeant and parrot strolled into the meeting.
Everyone stopped talking. Everyone stopped eating.

Sir Robert looked the pair of them up and down
With a dangerous look in his eye. He said, "Brown,

I've seen some things in the Force, my *word* upon it,
But never once a Sergeant with a shoulder with a bird upon i

Take it off at once, you ridiculous clown!"
"Shut your beak," said Sergeant Brown.

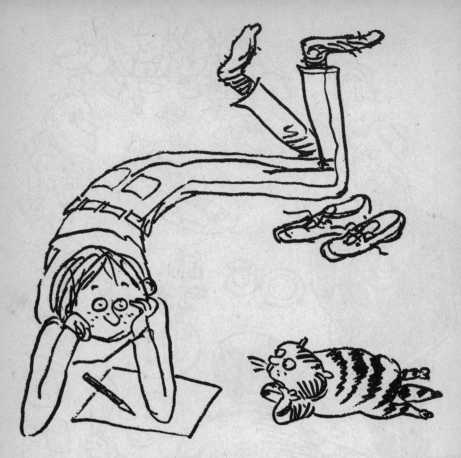

Some Days

I didn't find it interesting,
Listening,
I didn't find it interesting,
Talking,
So I left the house—I went miles and miles—
And I didn't find it interesting,
Walking.

I didn't find it interesting,
Reading,
I didn't find it interesting,
Writing,
So I left the house—I went miles and miles—
And that wasn't terribly
Exciting.

I watched my sister playing
Patience,
But I didn't find it interesting,
Scoring,
So I left the house—I went miles and miles—
And that was *extremely*
Boring.

I didn't find it interesting,
Telly,
There wasn't much on
That night,
So I sat in a chair and I went to sleep,
A dull old day
All right.

Some People

You can't tell some people anything.

I told my friend a secret.
"It dies with me," he said.
Then he dropped dead.

You can't tell some people anything.

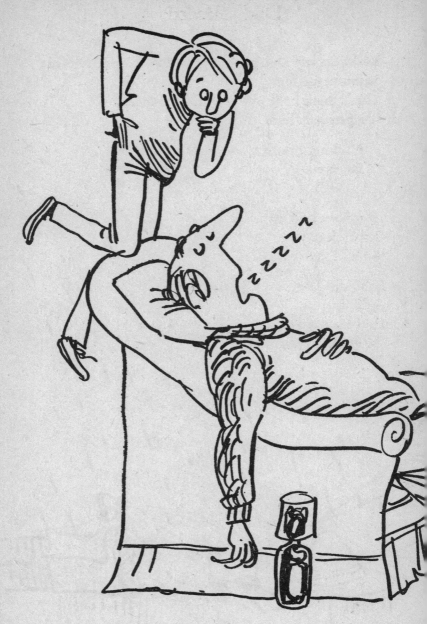

Dad's Beard

Last year my Dad grew a great big thick red beard:
Mum made him.
Can't think how in the world she managed
To persuade him.

  Nothing but hair
  Everywhere:
    Can't say I liked it at all.

But now he's shaved it,
I wonder:
Should he have saved it?

It's odd. Did Dad look better with his beard?
I doubt it.
But he certainly looks pretty weird
Without it.

  Nothing but face
  All over the place:
    Can't say I like it at all.

Uncle Joe's Jalopy

When you're riding in my Uncle Joe's jalopy,
Better hang on tight 'cos the roads are pretty choppy
When you're travelling in that car.

It's a dumpy little jumpy little bumpy little number
And it doesn't pay to sleep and it doesn't pay to slumber
And you'd best not go too far
When you're travelling in that car.

It's got holes in the roof the snow has snowed through,
Holes in the floor you can see the road through,
Holes in the dash the petrol's flowed through—
Pretty scary car!

It's got broken springs—brakes on the blink—
Wheels that wobble—fumes that stink—
And the windscreen's turned as black as ink
So you can't see where you are
When you're travelling in that car:
So you'd best not   go too   far!

But don't you *criticize* that jalopy
Or Uncle Joe will get mighty stroppy
'Cos he really likes that car!

When he's at the wheel of that old bone-shaker
He thinks he's a Grand Prix record-breaker—
He thinks he's a motor star!

When he bangs round corners on two square wheels,
Folks on the pavement take to their heels
'Cos they don't feel as safe as Uncle Joe feels
When he's travelling in that car:

And as for me, I can't wait for the day
When the wheels fall off and the roof blows away
And Uncle Joe will just have to say,
"Well, that's the end of that car:
It really can't   go too   far!"

I Don't Like You

If I were the Prime Minister of Britain
And you were a snail
I'd be most careful walking round my garden
Not to disturb your trail.

If I were a snail and you were the Prime Minister
It wouldn't be like that.
You'd tramp around in your expensive boots
And squash me flat.

I Like You

When you're unkind
You don't mean to be.
And when you're kind
You couldn't care less
Whether or not
You're seen to be.

What I like about you
Is how you know what's cooking
In somebody else's mind.
You do the best you can
And you just don't care
Who's looking.

Ghosts

That's right. Sit down and talk to me.
What do you want to talk about?

Ghosts. You were saying that you believe in them.
Yes, they exist, without a doubt.

What, bony white nightmares that rattle and glow?
No, just spirits that come and go.

I've never heard such a load of rubbish.
Never mind, one day you'll know.

What makes you so sure?

I said:
What makes you so sure?

Hey,
Where did you go?

Six White Skeletons

Deep deep down in the sea in the deep sea darkness
where the big fish
flicker and loom
and the weeds are alive
like hair

the hull of the wreck
grates in the sand:
in and out
of its ribs of steel—
only the long eel
moves there.

Down in the engine-room
six white skeletons:

only the long eel
moves there.

Nutter

The moon's a big white football,
The sun's a pound of butter.
The earth is going round the twist
And I'm a little nutter!

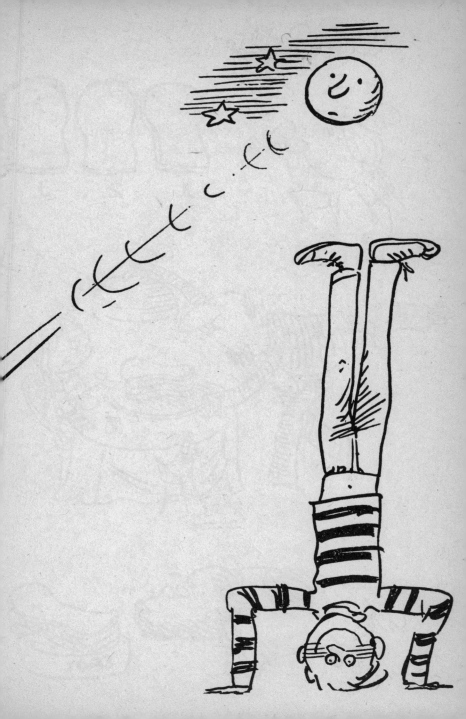

1.   2.   3.

SPOT

If You're No Good at Cooking

If you're no good at cooking,
Can't fry or bake,

Here's something you
Can always make. Take

Three very ordinary
Slices of bread:

Stack the second
On the first one's head.

Stack the third
On top of that.

There! Your three slices
Lying pat.

So what have you got?
A BREAD SANDWICH,

That's what!
Why not?

A Visit to the Aquarium

Watching the conger eel

(a three foot slice of muscle,
a blue blade of steel
that cast a motionless shadow
on the lit glass floor of its cell)

I saw the sudden whiplash ripple
of its whole body
that crashed the plunging water
as it swallowed
and then was still

And I thought of my friend Dave Dirt,
too fast to live, too young to die,
who
sudden as lightning

SWIPED

the Last Cake
at Phyllis Willis's birthday party!

Dave and the conger eel:
neither of them like to leave
anything to chance . . .
or to anyone
else.

Snoozing by the Boozer

All day outside the boozer snores
The boozer-keeper's big brown dog
And carefully each boozer-user
Coming to or from the boozer
Steps around the shaggy snoozer,
  Dumped there like a log.

It chanced a fellow named de Souza
(An American composer)
Once was passing by the boozer
Humming to himself a Blues. A
Dog-enthuser, this de Souza,
So he halted by the boozer.
With his stick he poked the snoozer.
"Big brown dog," he said, "say who's a
  Good boy then?" This shows a

Lack of knowledge of the boozer-
Keeper's dog. It is a bruiser,
  Not a dreamy dozer.

Up it sprang and ate de Souza,
The American composer.
He is dead, the dog-enthuser.

Don't poke dogs outside the boozer.
You are bound to be the loser.

Frankie and Johnny are Useless

Now, Frankie's a nimble showjumper,
Like Princess Anne over the course,
But she jumped the waterjump one day
And that waterjump drowned her horse—

It was her thing
But she did it wrong.

Well, Johnny's a brilliant goalie,
I've not seen a better one yet,
But he let through so many goals one game,
Bust a hole in the back of the net—

It was his thing
But he did it wrong.

Now, Frankie's a dab hand at cooking,
She was cooking the family treat,
But she cooked it so well you just couldn't tell
The potatoes from the meat—

It was her thing
But she did it wrong.

Well, Johnny's a dazzling skater,
On skates he's as good as they come,
But he fell over so many times one night,
Should have worn skates on his bum—

It was his thing
But he did it wrong.

Now, Frankie is *good* on the cello,
You really should hear Frankie play,
But she played it so badly the audience left
And the cello walked away—

It was her thing
But she did it wrong.

Well, Johnny's a master chess player,
Yes, Johnny's amazing at chess,
But he hit that board so hard with his knee,
Where the pieces were—anyone's guess—

It was his thing
But he did it wrong.

Now, I've written a dim little poem,
I've sung you a boring old song,
Told so many lies, can't believe my eyes,
And I've gone on far too long—

Well, it's my thing
But I've done it wrong!

The Fate of the Supermarket Manager

There once was a Supermarket manager
And a very happy manager was he.

He *reduced the prices*
Of the lollies and the ices!
He made *huge cuts*
On the fruit and nuts!
Corn-flakes, steaks
And home-bake cakes,
Dog-food, detergent,
Devil-fish, dates,
He sold at *half*
The market rates!
And (so my sister
Said to me)
He put stickers
On the knickers
In the Lingerie
Saying:
Prices down
By 15p!
And he wrote, as a treat,
By the luncheon meat:
YOU'D HAVE TO BE BARMY
TO BUY THIS SALAMI
So he gave it away
For free!

Yes, there once was a Supermarket manager
And a very happy manager was he.

What a bloke!

He was much admired.

The shop went broke.

He was fired.

Say Cheese

Cheese!

At Christmas the STILTON
Was spilt on the Wilton,
The rare CAMEMBERT
Was as fine as can be,
But at New Year the GRUYERE
It just went straight through yer,
The CHEDDAR was bedder
But as for the BRIE,

Aaaaaaaagh! And the PORT SALUD!
Swallow one morsel, you
Kept to your bed
For a week and a day,
And if you tried WENSLEYDALE
You quite *immensely*'d ail,
Hospital-bound
Till they wheeled you away!

No better was EMMENTHAL,
Sour and inclement, all
Cratered and pocked
Like a view of the moon!
And while some are crazy
For creamed BEL PAESE,
Myself, I'd eat forcemeat
Or horsemeat as soon!

The LEICESTER was best o'
'The bunch, but the rest o'
Them curled up your stomach.
Though GLOUCESTER (times two)
And jaundiced old CHESHIRE
I'd·taste under pressure,
Nothing would get me,
No, nothing would get me,
But nothing would get me
To try DANISH BLUE!

The Frozen Man

Out at the edge of town
where black trees

crack their fingers
in the icy wind

and hedges freeze
on their shadows

and the breath of cattle,
still as boulders,

hangs in rags
under the rolling moon,

a man is walking
alone:

on the coal-black road
his cold

feet
ring

and
ring.

Here in a snug house
at the heart of town

the fire is burning
red and yellow and gold:

you can hear the warmth
like a sleeping cat

breathe softly
in every room.

When the frozen man
comes to the door,

let him in,
let him in,
let him in.

Lies

When we are bored
My friend and I
Tell
Lies.

It's a competition: the prize
Is won by the one
Whose lies
Are the bigger size.

We really do:
That's true.
But there isn't a prize:
That's lies.

Blue Wish

When the gas-fire glows
  It tingles with a
    Low
    Blue light.
    It
Dances with a slow
  Flicker of wishing:
Wish I may,
  Wish I might

Have a blue wish
  Always burning,
Noon,
  Burning,
    Night.

Our Hamster's Life

Our hamster's life:
there's not much
to it,
not much
to it.

He presses his pink nose
to the door of his cage
and decides for the fifty six
millionth time
that he can't get
through it.

Our hamster's life;
there's not much
to it,
not much
to it.

It's about the most boring
life in the world,
if he only
knew it.
He sleeps and he drinks and he eats.
He eats and he drinks and he sleeps.

He slinks and he dreeps.
He eats.

This process
he repeats.

Our hamster's life:
there's not much
to it,
not much
to it.

You'd think it would drive him bonkers,
going round and round on his wheel.
It's certainly driving me bonkers,

watching him
do it.

But he may be thinking:
"That boy's life,
there's not much
to it,
not much
to it:

watching a hamster go round on a wheel.
It's driving me bonkers if he only knew it,

watching him
watching me
do it."

Watch Your French

When my mum tipped a panful of red-hot fat
Over her foot, she did quite a little chat,
And I won't tell you what she said
But it wasn't:
"Fancy that!
I must try in future to be far more careful
With this red-hot scalding fat!"

When my dad fell over and landed—splat!—
With a trayful of drinks (he'd tripped over the cat)
I won't tell you what he said
But it wasn't:
"Fancy that!
I must try in future to be far more careful
To step *round* our splendid cat!"

MON DIEU!

When Uncle Joe brought me a cowboy hat
Back from the States, the dog stomped it flat,
And I won't tell you what I said
But Mum and Dad yelled:
"STOP THAT!
Where did you learn that appalling language?
Come on. Where?"

"I've no idea," I said,
"No idea."

Bluebells and Penguins

The day we found the lady
Crying in the wood
We tried to comfort her
As best we could
But just what she was crying for
We never understood:

Weeping among the beechleaves and the bluebells.

The day we saw the old man
Cackling at the zoo
We had a laugh along with him
The way you do
But just what he was laughing at
We never had a clue:

Chuckling among the pythons and the penguins!

Now penguins aren't that funny
And bluebells aren't that sad
But sometimes you feel really good
And sometimes you feel bad.
Sometimes you feel sky-high happy,
Sometimes lost and low,
And why on earth you feel like that
Sometimes
      you
        don't
          know!

Jeremy Mobster Lobster

In the black salt-sluices of the weed-choked rockpool
  With fish-eyes, garbage, vanishing fry
And rusting backbones in the squelchy tunnel
  That opens and closes like a murderous eye
  As the tide slurs in and the tide drawls out
  And the grinding shingle churns about,
              With his horrible claws
                  For company
              Sits Jeremy Mobster Lobster,
              The meanest fish in the sea.

              The meanest fish,
              The uncleanest fish,
              The obscenest fish in the sea.

Watch out, shrimp! Better say your prayers!
Down in the rockpool
Jeremy's God.
Better have a little bit of
Dead fish ready
For that big mean old
Arth-ro-pod!

Pay up, crayfish! Pay up, crab!
Shell out for Jeremy's
Protection racket.
It'll cost you a packet
But don't complain

Or you might not grow
That shell again . . .

His wavering, wobbly, flickering eye-stalks
Scrape round the walls of his bony cave
And you'll find no cover in the wallowing darkness,
You won't be hidden by the blackest wave
For there with the barnacles studding his back
And you in mind as his next big snack,
With his horrible claws
For company
Sits Jeremy Mobster Lobster,
The meanest fish in the sea.

The meanest fish,
The uncleanest fish,
The obscenest fish in the sea.

All of the Morning

I've been staring
  all of the morning
    out at the endlessly
      falling rain

that drowns the garden
  in tank after tank full
    of see-through tears without
      anger or pain,

joy or sorrow,
  shock or laughter,
    only the helplessly
      falling rain

that springs pink worms
  from their tight dark prison
    and sticks the snails
      to the bumpy wall

with what appear to be
  squiggles of stretched, spat,
    chewed-up chewing-gum.
      Let it fall,

flooding the cones
   of lilac, laburnum's
      yellow bells
         that ring their small

tune of the sun
   in the soaked grey morning,
      let it fall.
         If I weren't me,

the helpless rain
   that falls forever
      I could be,
         quite easily.

Rabbiting Off

Now you see me,
Now you don't,
First you'll miss me,
Then you won't.

Spoken my story,
Sung my song.
I've been round here
All day long

For a yell and a whisper,
Shout and a cough,
Rabbiting on
And sounding off.

Sounding off
And rabbiting on:
I was here
And now I'm . . .